A Horseman's Heart

Horsemen of Cross Roads Farm ~ Book 1

MYRA JOHNSON

Dedication

For my brother Ralph, horseman and saddle maker extraordinaire.

For the gentle horses and dedicated volunteers serving at therapeutic riding centers everywhere, especially my human and equine friends at JoyRide Center Therapeutic Horsemanship Program and SIRE, Houston's Therapeutic Equestrian Center. I miss all of you so much!

And with immense gratitude to God for this native Texan's opportunity to enjoy eight years living in beautiful North Carolina before bringing us back home to Texas.

Chapter One

Saving Gem was by far the most beautiful work he'd ever done.

Giving him up might be the hardest thing he'd ever do.

Kip Lorimer tapped the telephone number displayed on the website he'd come across last week, then lifted his cell phone to his ear.

"Cross Roads Farm." The lilting voice took him by surprise. The woman he'd spoken with a few days ago had sounded a little more mature.

"Uh, Mrs. Cross?"

"She isn't available just now."

No reason Kip should suddenly feel so off balance, but he did. Probably a bad case of nerves after that near-miss at the supermarket last week. He pulled his thoughts together. "Just tell her I'll be headed that way tomorrow with the horse I talked to her about. I should get there sometime late Tuesday."

"Okay." Something ripped, like paper tearing off a notepad. "Tuesday, you said?"

"North Carolina's a long drive from Texas."

Silence. "You're bringing us a horse all the way from Texas?"

"Uh, yeah."

"Sorry, it's just that our horse donations usually come from local people." The woman gave a soft laugh. "Do you need directions?"

"Got it covered."

"And your name and number, please?"

"Lorimer. Kip Lorimer." Kip pressed his lips together. This wasn't the time to explain that by noon tomorrow, he planned to trash this phone and buy a new one. With a new number. "Tell you what. I'll call again as I get closer."

"Okay, I'll give my mother the message. Have a safe trip."

"Thanks, ma'am." Kip ended the call with those gentle words echoing through his brain: *Have a safe trip.*

And he hadn't even gotten her name.

Forget it, man. He didn't need any woman—even one with a voice as airy as spun sugar—getting under his skin. Now or ever.

He finished packing his saddle-making tools and locked them in the trunk behind his pickup cab. After stowing the rest of his meager belongings in the front section of his two-horse trailer, he checked on Gem in the corral before grabbing what shut-eye he could on this muggy June night.

Morning came all too soon. "Into the trailer, boy. Time to head out." He laid the lead rope across the flyspecked gray's withers and patted the muscled rump. The horse nickered and stepped easily into the trailer.

Moving around to the window, Kip reached through the opening and clipped the trailer tie to Gem's halter. Before he could unsnap the lead rope and pull it through,

Gem was already attacking the hay net like the poor horse hadn't eaten in weeks.

Three years or thirty, abandonment was a hard thing to forget.

Kip rubbed Gem's ear with affection and then climbed in behind the wheel of his battered white pickup. With one last look at the rented doublewide he'd called home since settling here almost four years ago, he steered the pickup down the graveled lane. One more stop before hitting the highway.

About seven miles down the two-lane farm road, Kip pulled up to the T Bar J Ranch security gate and pressed the intercom button. Seconds later, Tom Jacobs's husky voice greeted him. "Howdy, Kip! Come on through. I'll meet you at the barn."

The black iron gates swung open, and Kip drove through, slowing to admire Tom's herd of sleek quarter horses and thoroughbreds. Tom Jacobs waved Kip to a halt in front of the massive gray-and-white barn. Stepping out of the pickup, Kip accepted the big man's firm handshake.

"So you're really doing this, huh?" Tom hooked his thumbs into his front jeans pockets. "You'll sure be missed around these parts."

Kip tucked in his chin. In one lithe movement, he hoisted himself up and over the wheel well. Folding back a canvas cover, he revealed the custom reining saddle he'd been working on for the past two months.

A long, low whistle sliced the morning air. Tom leaned in to run an admiring hand along the wild rose tooling on the skirt and stirrup leather. "That is as fine a piece of saddle-making as I've ever seen."

With a nod of thanks, Kip hefted the saddle and passed it down to Tom, then hopped to the ground and followed the man into the immaculate tack room. Familiar smells of horse and leather filled Kip's nostrils, smells he'd grown up with, smells he cherished. He breathed in slowly and tried to imagine owning his own ranch someday. Raising a fine herd of horses. Maybe even getting married and starting a family.

Scratch the last part. Horses, you could trust. Women? Not so much.

With an almost reverential sigh, Tom Jacobs set the saddle on a rack in the center of the room. "Montana's gonna look mighty spiffy in this get-up. What do I owe you, son?"

Kip pulled a wrinkled invoice from his shirt pocket and silently handed it to Tom. He'd need every cent of his profits to cover this trip to North Carolina, then find somewhere new to settle for a while. It was time to clear out of Texas once and for all.

Tom scanned the bill with a smirk. "How many times have I told you? You're way undercharging for work this fine. Let's go to my office and I'll write you a check."

Kip welcomed the coolness of the air-conditioned room. He dropped onto the edge of a maroon leather chair. "I appreciate all the business you've given me, the customers you've sent my way."

"My pleasure." Tom ripped the check from his checkbook and passed it across the desk. "Added on a little bonus. You earned it."

Kip's throat closed. A thousand dollars more than the price he'd quoted. "This is too much—"

"No arguments." Tom leaned back, his chair rocking gently. "You got a long, hard haul ahead. You'll need some seed money once you get where you're going."

"But—"

"Just say thank you and get on outta here. Maybe you can make Birmingham by suppertime." Tom stood and strode to the door.

Kip folded the check in half and tucked it into his shirt pocket. Tom Jacobs was a good man, a man of integrity. A man who knew how to treat both animals and people like they deserved a measure of respect.

A man who made Kip miss his dad more than ever.

Lips pressed together, he pushed up from the chair and offered his hand. "Thanks. More than I can say."

Sheridan Cross laced her arms across her sky-blue cotton sweater and frowned. "I can't imagine what's keeping my mom."

The plump Charlotte real estate agent wiped a sheen of sweat off his upper lip. "Why don't we wait inside? The house is vacant, but I'm pretty sure they left the air on."

"Thanks, but I'd rather not." Sheridan strained for a glimpse of her mother's silver Chevy Tahoe. If Mom didn't get here soon, Sheridan would be late returning to school for this afternoon's end-of-year wrap-up meeting.

The agent moved deeper into the shade of an old magnolia tree. "Maybe you should try phoning her again."

"Mom never answers her cell phone if she's driving. I'm sure she's on her way." Or else in a ditch somewhere or trapped beneath the wheels of a semi . . .

Cool it, Sher. Mom is fine, just running a little late.

Sunlight reflected off the windshield of an approaching vehicle. Sheridan breathed a sigh of relief. "There's my mom now."

The silver SUV drew to a stop across the street. Linda

Cross set her sunglasses atop her silver-blond pixie cut and beamed a smile as she stepped from the car. "Sorry I'm late, honey. I ran into some road construction on the way into town."

"I was getting a little worried."

Reaching the sidewalk, Mom pulled Sheridan into a quick hug. "You worry way too much, young lady."

"Can't help it." Sheridan's mouth quirked. Grabbing her mother's hand, she drew her over to the tree where the real estate agent waited. "Mr. Vasilis, I'd like you to meet my mother, Linda Cross."

"My pleasure, ma'am." He wiped his right hand on his slacks before accepting a handshake. His glance darted between Sheridan and her mother, and an appreciative grin spread his lips. "Gracious me, you two could pass for twin sisters!"

Sheridan's mother winked at her daughter. "Thanks. We get that a lot."

"Shall we go inside and look around?" Mr. Vasilis started toward the front porch of the single-story brick house.

Mom grabbed Sheridan's elbow. "Honey, are you thinking of moving out of your townhouse?"

"No, Mom. I mean, yes, but—" Sheridan heaved a groan. "Just look at the house, and then we'll talk, okay?"

Mom gasped. "Sher! Have you met somebody? And you never told me—"

"No, it's *nothing* like that!" Sheridan closed her eyes briefly. Dating was the *last* thing on her mind. She drew her mother aside and lowered her voice. "You know how I worry about you living alone on the farm. I thought if I found us a nice little affordable house in town, I could convince you to move in with me. Now that Xena's full-grown, she's too big for my place anyway, and—"

Mom took a giant step backward. "I can't believe you'd suggest such a thing! Cross Roads Farm was your dad's dream. I'll carry on our work if for no other reason than that."

Sheridan forced a swallow down her aching throat. "I know how much the farm means to you, how much it meant to Dad. But now that he's gone, I can't stand the thought of you living out there by yourself."

Mom glanced toward the real estate agent, then leaned closer until she and Sheridan were touching foreheads. "Honey, you've got to stop dwelling on the past."

A grating sigh tore through Sheridan's chest. "Am I so wrong to want you close, where I know you're safe?"

"I'm perfectly safe at the farm. And it isn't like I'm completely isolated. Manuelo comes every day to handle the barn chores, and now Nathan's home from college for the summer. Plus the class instructors and volunteers—"

"But it's not the same with Dad gone." Sheridan gave her mother a pleading look.

Mom leveled her gaze at Sheridan for a long and painful three seconds before swiveling to address Mr. Vasilis. By the time she spoke, her sober expression had morphed into a mask of Southern sweetness. "You *must* forgive us for taking up your valuable time, but my daughter and I have had a *teensy* misunderstanding. I'm afraid we have to go."

"But you haven't seen the house." The red-faced man trotted toward them. "Three amply-sized bedrooms, newly remodeled kitchen—"

"Perhaps another time." Mom was already hustling Sheridan around to the driver's side of her red Prius.

"Mom—"

"Go finish up at school, honey. And forget this nonsense." Mom nudged her into the seat, and then leaned in and smacked a noisy kiss on her cheek. "And try praying for a change. That's the best antidote for worry I know."

If only it were that easy. Shoulders drooping, Sheridan cast her mother a reluctant smile. "At least have a quick lunch with me since you're in town?"

"Only if you promise—" An electronic rendition of "Sweet Caroline" drifted from Mom's open car window. "Hold on, better get that." She jogged across the street and retrieved her cell phone.

Sheridan caught her mother's first few words, something about Nathan, Sheridan's younger brother. Mom's eyebrows shot up. Her gaze met Sheridan's and she gave her head a tiny shake. "There's been an accident. Nathan's in the hospital."

Both Kip's gas tank and his stomach were running on empty by the time he stopped at a mom-and-pop convenience store near downtown Kingsley, North Carolina. With the pickup refueled and a boxed ham sandwich and canned cola to tide him over, he checked his directions once more and headed on through town. Soon he spotted the blue-and-yellow sign at the Cross Roads Farm entrance. No fancy security gate, just a wide aluminum ranch gate standing open like a welcoming smile . . . kind of like that sweet voice on the phone the other evening.

Have a safe trip. The words—and the voice they belonged to—had played through his mind like a haunting melody through two long days on the road. More than once he'd found himself trying to picture the face behind the words. And more than once he'd stomped on that impulse like a boot heel smashing a cockroach. Such thoughts were only asking for trouble, the kind of trouble he'd been avoiding for half his life.

He steered the pickup across the cattle guard and followed a one-lane gravel road toward a farmhouse and a big yellow barn with white trim. The tires bounced through muddy ruts from a recent rain, but otherwise the farm looked well kept.

Parking next to the barn, Kip shut off the engine and jumped out to look around. Didn't appear to be a soul on the place. Not even a light on in the main house, and the sun already dipped low in the western sky. He'd called earlier when he'd stopped for lunch outside Atlanta—half hoping and half dreading the younger Ms. Cross would answer—but only reached voicemail.

Rustling sounds inside the barn drew his attention. He ambled around the pickup as a broad-chested brown dog bounded out of the shadowy building. Kip froze while the dog sized him up. Apparently deciding the stranger wasn't a threat, the dog wagged his tail and sniffed Kip's outstretched hand. Kip knelt to scratch the dog behind the ears. "Some guard dog you are. What's your name, fella?"

The dog answered with a wet tongue across Kip's face. Wiping dog slobber off his cheek, Kip chuckled and moseyed into the barn. "Hello? Anybody here?"

A short, stocky man carrying a pitchfork moved into view beneath a flickering overhead fluorescent. "You looking for *Señora* Cross?"

Kip edged forward. "Yeah. She's expecting me."

"*No está aquí.*"

Growing up in Texas, Kip knew just enough Spanish to

get by. Barely. So the lady wasn't home. "*Cuándo . . .* uh . . . when will she be back?"

"Sorry, my English is okay but I forget. *Señora* Cross's son is hurt. She is at the hospital." The man looked past Kip. "Ah, you are bringing the horse? I have a stall ready."

Kip let out a relieved sigh. The last thing Gem needed was another night in that cramped trailer. "Thanks. I'll get him."

After introducing horse and dog, Kip walked Gem around to familiarize him with his new surroundings, then led the horse into the barn. The stable hand—Manuelo, he said his name was—appeared with a flake of hay and a scoop of oats and nodded toward the last stall on the left. The scent and rustle of fresh shavings as Gem stepped through the stall door provided added assurance that the horse would have a good home here.

Now came the hard part. Saying goodbye.

Driving her mother's Tahoe, Sheridan slowed as the high beams reflected off the taillights of a horse trailer parked near the barn. The back of her neck prickled. "Mom? Somebody's here."

Mom yawned and rubbed her eyes. "Are we home already?"

Sheridan steered the SUV into the garage, then shut off the engine and tugged her cell phone from her purse. Why would anybody be at the farm this late at night? And why wasn't Beau out there barking his fool head off?

A deep-throated woof sounded in her ear. If Beau wouldn't fulfill his guard dog duties, at least Sheridan had

Xena. The imposing black Great Dane would surely intimidate the visitor right off the property.

Mom seemed more awake by the time she joined Sheridan outside the garage. "Oh, no. With everything else happening, I completely forgot." She marched toward the barn.

Sheridan let Xena out of the backseat and jogged to catch up. "Forgot what? Mom—"

A man in a cowboy hat strode around the rear of the horse trailer, and Sheridan's breath stopped for a moment. Tall, broad-shouldered, an easy swagger to his gait—she might have thought him attractive under any other circumstances.

But not at ten o'clock at night, with no one close enough to hear two women scream. She tightened her grip on her cell phone.

It didn't help when Xena loped right up to the stranger, tail whipping back and forth and tongue wagging out the side of her mouth like she'd known the guy forever. He barely had time to pat the Dane on the head before Xena and Beau took off for some quality doggy rough-housing.

"Mrs. Cross?" The cowboy's gaze shifted between Sheridan and her mother. He doffed his hat, revealing close-cropped, dust-colored hair with a distinct hat ring. The mercury vapor pole light next to the barn cast eerie shadows across his face. "I'm Kip Lorimer."

Of course. The guy who'd called Sunday evening about bringing the horse.

Still, he was a stranger.

"Glad you made it safely." Mom offered her hand. "I'm Linda Cross, and this is my daughter, Sheridan. Sorry I wasn't here when you arrived, but my son took a bad spill from his horse yesterday. We've just come from the hospital."

"That's too bad. I hope he'll be okay." Same Texas drawl, same husky voice. He flicked a glance toward Sheridan that made her insides do strange things.

"No permanent damage, for which we're all thankful," Mom answered. "Did you have any trouble finding us?"

"Drove right to the place. Manuelo helped me get Gem settled in a stall. I left Gem's vet records and the transfer-of-ownership papers in the tack room for you. I was just heading out."

"Already?" Concern etched Mom's face. "Do you have a place to stay?"

Sheridan's stomach tightened. She gave her mother a meaningful stare.

The cowboy shrugged. "Thought I'd pull into a roadside park somewhere. My trailer's set up for camping."

Sheridan pasted on a smile. "I've seen a nice little park just after you get back on the highway. It has restrooms, vending machines—"

"Don't be silly." Mom gave her head a small shake and turned a warm smile toward the cowboy. "Why don't you park your trailer right here by the barn? You can hook up to our electricity, use our water, whatever you need."

"*Mom.*" The word came out in a whispered plea.

Her mother ignored her. "Look, Mr. Lorimer, it's late, and I'm sure you're as tired as we are. Besides, before we finalize the paperwork, I'll need to do a series of tests to make sure Gem really is therapy horse material—not that I expect he wouldn't be after what you told me on the phone."

The cowboy twisted his hat brim. "Well, if you wouldn't mind . . ."

"Just pull up next to the barn here, and when you get settled, come knock on the kitchen door and I'll have a plate of food for you."

Sheridan heaved a resigned sigh. At least Mom wouldn't be alone tonight with a stranger camping on the property. Learning her brother would be out of commission for several weeks, Sheridan had hurriedly cancelled a teacher enrichment class so she could stay at the farm with Mom and help with the summer equine therapy sessions. A new batch of volunteers would arrive for training this Saturday, then eight weeks of classes would start next Tuesday.

She only hoped the cowboy didn't plan on sticking around that long.

While her mother prepared a plate of reheated leftovers for the cowboy and handed him a chilled bottle of water, Sheridan finished cleaning up the kitchen. Then she kissed her mother good night and trudged upstairs with Xena. What good was owning a big, black, scary-looking canine if the silly thing couldn't be counted upon to wreak fear and trembling upon strangers in cowboy hats?

"My next dog will be a well-trained Rottweiler." Sheridan pointed a stern finger toward the plush doggy cushion she'd brought along for Xena. "And no, you are *not* sleeping on the bed with me tonight."

Without even the energy to shower before slipping into her sleep tee, she turned back the quilted spread in her childhood bedroom and crawled between the cool sheets.

It had been a grueling two days sitting with Nathan at the hospital. The broken collar bone, fractured wrist, and mild concussion posed the least of his problems. The real issue was a cracked neck vertebra—a "minor cervical compression fracture," the doctor had called it. And for the first twenty-four hours, Nathan had little or no sensation in his arms and legs. Feeling had begun to return this afternoon, and by the time Sheridan and her mother left, Nathan was wiggling his fingers and toes and flirting with the nurses.

It could have been so much worse.

Tears sprang into Sheridan's eyes. She bit down on her lower lip and stared into the darkness. *God, why can't You protect my family?*

Chapter Two

Lemon pepper chicken, roasted veggies, warm garlic bread. The food tasted so good that Kip almost forgot to swallow. Rather than eat in his cramped makeshift trailer camper— basically the narrow dressing-room section furnished with a foam mattress, cooler, camp stove, and portable camping toilet—he'd carried the meal into the barn and sat outside Gem's stall on a hay bale. "Yep, I think you're gonna like it here, boy."

Except it was clear from the get-go that Mrs. Cross's daughter—Sheridan, if he caught her name right—wasn't too thrilled about having Kip stick around. Well, he'd be on his way soon enough. So what if the woman that sweet voice on the phone belonged to was ten times prettier than he'd imagined?

The last bite of garlic bread stuck in his throat. If *she* didn't keep butting into his life and messing things up, maybe things could be different. He'd actually started to like the Nacogdoches area. Through contacts like Tom Jacobs, he'd established a fair reputation among the locals as an expert horse trainer and skilled saddle maker.

Now he had to start over. Again.

Sleep came hard that night—too many memories competed with visions of the life he'd never have. He'd just stepped out of his trailer the next morning when he spied Mrs. Cross ambling toward him, the plump chocolate Lab at her heels. "Mornin', ma'am. Thanks again for the food. It hit the spot."

"You're more than welcome. I thought you might—"

A door slammed and Mrs. Cross's daughter jogged toward them. She looked soft and sleepy-eyed, her shirt buttoned all catawampus and her short-short blond hair mashed up on one side like she'd slept funny and hadn't taken time to comb it.

Kip's stomach dipped. He suddenly felt extra-conscious of the whiskers he hadn't shaved since leaving Texas.

Mrs. Cross gave her daughter an odd look. "I thought you'd be sleeping in, Sheridan."

"That's okay, Mom. I thought you might need some help." Sheridan cast a pursed-lip smile at Kip.

Mrs. Cross raised one eyebrow. "If you want to be of *help*, sweetheart, why don't you fetch Mr. Lorimer a mug of coffee?" She turned to Kip. "And since I'm guessing your trailer isn't big enough to include shower facilities, you're welcome to use our guest bathroom."

Sheridan's panicked stare told Kip this offer was definitely not okay with her—and for some crazy reason it pained him to think he caused such distress. "That's real nice of you, ma'am, but I've imposed long enough. If we could get started on those tests you talked about—"

"All in good time. But not before I whip you up a batch of my famous buckwheat blueberry pancakes."

"Bu–buckwheat . . ." If Kip were a dog, he'd have about a gallon of drool running down his chest. He swallowed hard. His stomach rumbled loud enough to be heard three counties away.

Sheridan Cross's deer-in-the-headlights look suddenly didn't matter. Kip had just decided to stay awhile longer.

Sheridan could barely control the quaver in her voice. "You don't even know this guy, Mom! How can you invite him into our home like he's a long-lost relative?"

"You can't order your entire life based on one horrible day, honey. You've got to learn to trust again." Nudging Beau aside, Mom stepped to the pantry for the pancake mix and griddle. "Where's Xena? Has she been out yet?"

"She crawled into my bed as soon as I got up and went right back to sleep. And it was nearly *two* days, Mother. The most terrifying forty hours of my life." Sheridan retrieved the egg carton and milk jug from the refrigerator. Since Mom clearly would not be talked out of this insanity, Sheridan might as well make herself useful.

A knock sounded on the back door. Sheridan sucked in a quick breath before unsticking her feet from the floor and propelling her unwilling hand to reach for the knob. With barely a glance, she waved the cowboy across the threshold. "Bathroom's down the hall on the left."

He smiled politely and scratched Beau behind the ears before heading through the kitchen. Sheridan held herself rigid until he disappeared around the corner, then released the air from her lungs in a whoosh. Her next inhalation carried the odor of man sweat, and ugly memories swept through her like a tidal wave.

"Sher?" Mom glanced over her shoulder. "You okay?"

She shivered. "I hate being so paranoid. But sometimes

you're so—so—*un*concerned that it makes me feel like I have to be extra cautious to compensate. If anything ever happened to you . . ."

Mom laid aside her wooden spoon and pressed Sheridan's face between her hands. "I wish you could see how God has *already* protected us, every day of our lives. We're alive. We're healthy and safe and well provided for."

Sheridan pulled away. "How can you say that? Dad's heart attack wasn't even a year ago, and now Nathan's in the hospital. He's so lucky, it's incredible. He could just as easily be paralyzed for life."

"Are you not listening to yourself?" Mom lifted misty eyes toward the ceiling and took up her spoon again to stir the pancake batter. "How can you doubt that it was God's protection, not luck, that saved Nathan from being hurt much worse than he was?"

Before Sheridan's retort could find its way to her lips, she busied herself adding fresh water to the dogs' bowl and filling two food dishes with kibble. God, luck—sometimes life seemed so horribly out of control that Sheridan didn't know where to place her trust.

Sounds from the bathroom ceased, and a few minutes later the cowboy strode into view. His tanned face was whisker-free now. His sandy-blond hair, still wet from the shower, looked two shades darker. The hat ring must be semi-permanent, because Sheridan could still make out the indentations at his temples.

Ruggedly handsome, she might even say. Corny description straight out of a romance novel, but the cowboy did clean up nicely.

"Help yourself to some coffee, Mr. Lorimer." Mom removed the first batch of pancakes from the griddle. "Do you take cream or sugar?"

"Black's fine. And you can call me Kip." He sidled over to the counter and selected a brown ceramic mug off the rack.

Sheridan hugged herself. "Kip. Is that short for anything?"

"Nope. Don't even have a middle name. It's just plain Kip." He peered at her with raised eyebrows and sipped his coffee.

"And you drove all the way here from Texas? What part of Texas are you from?" Sheridan was trying to be polite, really she was. But her pitch rose higher with every word.

Mom ladled more batter onto the griddle. "Stop giving our guest the third degree and set out some plates."

Steeling herself, Sheridan edged around the cowboy and collected three plates from the cupboard. He didn't smell like man sweat anymore, thank goodness. She wasn't sure the apple-scented shower gel suited him, but the masculine undertones of clean, wet skin did something unexpected to her senses.

The *tick-tick* of doggy toenails sounded in the front hall. Xena ambled into the kitchen and accepted the cowboy's back scratch before joining Beau for their breakfast.

"That is one mighty big dog," Kip remarked. "You could almost put a saddle on her."

"About all she's good for." Sheridan laid flatware and napkins beside the plates and then cast a withering glance in the dogs' direction. "Obviously, Xena and Beau are both worthless as watchdogs."

"Xena? Like in that old TV show about the warrior princess?" Kip chortled.

Mom carried a platter of pancakes to the table. "More

like a pussycat princess, if you ask me. Sher, how about some butter and syrup?"

If not for Mom's polite chitchat, breakfast would have been even more strained. *Strong, silent type* certainly applied to this cowboy.

Except his eyes sure lit up when Mom asked him about the horse he'd brought. "Gem's a rescue horse. Found him three years ago—ribs poking out, sores covering his hide like someone had taken potshots at him with a pellet gun."

Mom gasped. "How could anyone be so cruel?"

"The owner was losing his land, couldn't afford the feed and vet bills anymore."

Pancakes and coffee swirled in Sheridan's stomach. "That's no excuse. He could have found the horse another home."

"This raises an important question." Mom dabbed a napkin to her lips. "Do you have legal title to Gem?"

"First thing I saw to. Once I convinced the owner I'd be getting Gem proper vet care and nursing him back to health, the man was plenty happy to sign him over to me." Kip took a long swig of his coffee. "Best investment of time and money I ever made. That Gem is one sweet horse."

Mom rested her hand on Kip's arm in a tender gesture that twisted Sheridan's heart. "Then why are you giving him up?"

The man's face closed off again. "Because it's time." He eased his chair away from the table. "Thank you kindly for the breakfast. If you don't mind, I'd like to finish up our business, say my goodbyes to Gem, and hit the road."

"What's your hurry?" Sheridan burst out, surprising herself. Maybe it was the man's obvious affinity for horses and dogs or maybe the lonely look in his eyes . . . or possibly just the way his fresh-from-the-shower glow reminded her of Daddy. Whatever it was, *something* about him had temporarily breached her defenses and crept into the hidden places of her heart. "I mean, do you have someplace else to be?"

He cast her a wary look. "Not exactly."

Okay, so she was acting completely out of character. But Beau and Xena both seemed to like the guy—here they were beside him, tails sweeping the floor and "feed me" looks gracing their big brown eyes as they cast hungry glances toward his syrup-smeared pancake plate. And didn't they say that if a dog made up to someone, he must be a good person?

Sheridan's lips flattened. Sam, the German shepherd they'd owned sixteen years ago, never would make friends with the Finstons. That alone should have clued them in.

The thought of the Finstons was enough to jar some sense back into Sheridan's cowboy-befuddled brain. She crumpled her napkin in her lap and lowered her gaze. "I just meant that you can't rush off before my mother has a chance to test your horse and verify the paperwork."

Chapter Three

As Kip predicted, Gem passed every test with flying colors —a bombproof horse if there ever was one, as if the mistreatment had only made him stronger, more patient, more giving. Paperwork now in order, Kip returned the ballpoint to Mrs. Cross and looked past the woman to where her daughter stood at the sink filling the dishwasher. For that one brief moment over breakfast, he'd sensed Sheridan relaxing her guard.

Well, he couldn't let himself care. "Thanks again for your kind hospitality. I know Gem will have a good home here."

Mrs. Cross followed him out to the back porch. "You still haven't told us where you're headed."

If only he had a clue. Indecision, doubt, and the never-ending dread that *she'd* catch up with him again landed across his shoulders with the weight of a roping saddle.

"I get the impression you weren't planning on returning to Texas."

"Nope." He started across the yard.

Mrs. Cross matched his stride. "Then do you have work lined up? A place to live?"

His steps faltered for a hair's breadth. "Nope."

"Obviously you have horsemanship skills."

"Guess so." Kip dared a sideways glance at the woman.

"Summer is our busiest season here with the equine therapy classes. My son was planning to help while he's home from college for the summer, but now that's out of the question." Mrs. Cross drew up in front of him as they neared the barn. "I could sure use a good man with horse sense."

Kip tucked his thumbs into his belt loops. "Ma'am, you just met me. You don't know a thing about me—whether I'm prone to Saturday-night drinking binges or smoking in the barn or thievery or—"

The woman's gray-blue eyes darkened for a split second. She folded her arms at her waist. "Are you?"

"No, but—"

"Then you're hired. If you want the job, that is."

"*Mom?*"

Kip spun around and found himself staring into eyes as blue and wide as a high-desert Texas sky. He raised both hands and backed off. "I didn't come here lookin' for work. Our business is settled and—"

"I just offered you a job, Mr. Lorimer. Now, do you need the work or don't you?"

Kip ground his teeth while he weighed his answer. Linda Cross might be slight in build, but an inner strength shone in her unyielding stare—a look that said she could be trusted, that she cared. He rocked back on his boot heels. "Yes, ma'am, I think I'd like working for you."

Sheridan clamped a hand on her mother's arm. "I told you, Mom, I'm free to stay for the whole summer. I know the horses. I know the routine. I can handle anything Nathan would have done."

"Honey, you're forgetting Nathan will need some extra attention for a while, and there are things . . ." Mrs. Cross glanced up at Kip with a crooked smile. "Well, there are certain things I know my son would prefer another male assisted him with. I realize that isn't part of the job description you had in mind, but it would be a huge help."

Kip's belly tightened. He sure wasn't looking to be anyone's nursemaid. "What kind of help exactly?"

Mrs. Cross released a light laugh. "Nathan won't be a complete invalid, but he has a cast on his wrist and will have to wear a neck brace most of the summer, so he may need help dressing, showering, that kind of thing."

Kip ran a hand across the top of his head. He wished he hadn't left his Stetson in the trailer. He could use something to hold on to. "I guess that would be okay."

"Thank you!" Mrs. Cross pressed her palms together. "That's a huge load off my mind."

Sheridan huffed a sigh. "At least ask for his references, Mom."

Mrs. Cross rolled her eyes in a skyward glance. "Very well. Mr. Lorimer, what's your background with horses? Anyone we could contact for verification?"

"Well, ma'am, I learned to ride before I could walk. Traveled with my dad on the rodeo circuit for half my life. Learned from some of the best horsemen in the business. As for references," he went on, "most recently I gentled and saddle-broke a four-year-old thoroughbred for a man back in Nacogdoches named Tom Jacobs. I've also trained a few of his reining and cutting horses."

Sheridan tugged a cell phone from her front jeans pocket. "Do you have his number? I'd be happy to make the call." She shot her mother a butter-wouldn't-melt-in-my-mouth smile.

At Mrs. Cross's resigned nod, Kip rattled off the number and waited as Sheridan spoke with Tom. He found himself staring at those long, blue-jeaned legs and the way Sheridan cocked one hip out while she listened. With her free hand she absently finger-combed her short, golden waves while darting looks toward Kip with those mesmerizing ice-blue eyes. Eyes that could drill a hole right through to his soul if he let them.

"He gave you a glowing recommendation." Sheridan pocketed her phone and quirked a half-smile. "Guess you're hired."

"How can Mom be so—so—"

"Trusting?" Nathan Cross thumbed the TV volume control on his hospital bed remote.

"Exactly." Pacing in front of the window, Sheridan clawed the back of her neck. "I worry every day she's at the farm alone. And then she hires the first stranger who comes along."

"If I hadn't been so gung-ho about heading out cross-country with Jet practically the minute I got home . . ." Nathan fisted his right hand. Jet was their dad's prize-winning hunter-jumper, a spirited ink-black Warmblood gelding they kept separate from the therapy horses.

Sheridan paused to gaze at her dark-haired, dark-eyed brother, a younger version of their father just like Sheridan resembled Mom. Nathan also shared Dad's love of horses *and* his competitive nature. "Jet hadn't been ridden since you were home at Easter. You should have expected he'd be a teensy bit frisky."

"Believe me, I learned my lesson." Nathan caught Sheridan's hand and tugged until she plopped into the chair beside the bed. "You said this Kip person has references. Are you sure they're legit?"

Sheridan studied the swirls in the floor tiles. "He definitely has an amazing way with the animals—the horses, Beau and Xena, even the barn cats."

"A real horse whisperer-plus, eh? Then why so worried?"

"You should worry, too, since Mom asked him if he'd also help with your, uh, *males only* needs after you come home."

Nathan squeezed one eye shut. "Huh?"

"You know, all the stuff you might need help with that you'd rather your mother and sister weren't around for."

He whooshed out a breath. "Hadn't thought about that part yet."

"Mom's even letting him move into the caretaker's cottage. He'll be around twenty-four/seven." Sheridan yanked her hand from Nathan's and stood. The unpleasant memories she fought so hard to tamp down churned in her belly.

"That *is* big. No one's occupied the cottage since the Finstons."

Sheridan crossed her arms. "I don't like it, Nathan. I just don't like it."

"Looks like you don't have a choice." Nathan let his head sink into the pillow. "Maybe it's time to move on, huh?"

She shuddered. "You weren't there. You don't know how scary it was."

"I know how scared Dad and I were when we got home from the camping trip and couldn't find you or Mom anywhere."

Staring out the window, Sheridan massaged her wrists, remembering the tight, sticky, unyielding duct tape. "Why weren't we more suspicious of the Finstons? How could Mom and Dad have let them get so close?"

"Guess they had everybody fooled."

The door swung open and Mom breezed in. "Shopping's all done." She planted a gentle kiss on Nathan's forehead. "Is Sheridan letting you get any rest?"

"She was just telling me about this cowboy you've hired —supposedly to be my nursemaid? Shouldn't *I* have a say about who sees me in my skivvies?"

Mom huffed. "I didn't hire him *just* to help you. He's an expert horseman and a truly nice young man. By the way, I ran into your doctor at the nurses' station. He says you can go home tomorrow. I think we should move you to the downstairs guest room for the summer."

"Whatever. I just want to get out of here."

Mom checked her watch. "Speaking of getting out of here, I've got a ton of groceries and supplies in the back of the Tahoe. Sheridan, we should get going."

"What did you do, clean out the Costco shelves again?" Sheridan hugged her brother's good arm, careful not to jar his neck. "Hang in there for one more night. We'll be back to bail you out tomorrow."

Kip and Manuelo worked most of the day cleaning up the one-bedroom caretaker's cottage next to the barn. Looked like the only life forms that had occupied the place in years were insects, rodents, and the occasional raccoon or possum. At this rate, Kip might be spending at least another night or two in his trailer.

Twisting a tie around the top of another stuffed green trash bag, he recalled how Mrs. Cross had flapped an empty trash bag at Gem as part of her testing. The horse's only reaction was to tuck in his chin and thrust his ears forward. Then she'd popped an umbrella open near Gem's face, rolled a beach ball between his legs, draped a Hula-Hoop over his neck, clipped clothespins to his mane, and come at him with an empty wheelchair. Kip could tell the horse wasn't exactly thrilled with all the paraphernalia, but Gem held steady and offered little more than the occasional snort or quiver.

Manuelo emerged from the bedroom with a stack of dusty cardboard boxes. "For *Natividad*. I will take these to the big house."

"Thanks." Kip sure didn't plan on sticking around until Christmas—too risky staying in any one place for too long.

Manuelo, on the other hand, had been employed as the Crosses' stable hand for over fifteen years. He lived with his wife and four youngest kids in a white frame house about a half-mile down the road. His wife had a housecleaning business and occasionally cleaned for Mrs. Cross. The soft-spoken Latino had nothing but praise for the Crosses' kindness and generosity—although Kip hadn't needed a whole lot of convincing.

With the chocolate Lab dogging his every step, Kip headed out to the dumpster with another load of trash. Sheridan and her mother had driven into town earlier and left the Dane in the house. Kip had the feeling the big, black, "scary" Xena was pretty much spoiled rotten.

As Kip and Beau headed back to the cottage, the sound of tires on gravel caught the dog's attention and he took off running. The silver Tahoe eased around the curving driveway and stopped outside the garage. Mrs. Cross and her daughter climbed out and popped open the back.

Eyeing the cargo area bulging with boxes and bags, Kip ambled over. "Looks like y'all could use some help." He stepped up to heft a cardboard box at the same time Sheridan reached for it. As their forearms touched, he sensed her sudden tension.

"I can get this one." She held her ground until Kip backed off, then muscled the heavy box out of the SUV.

Stubborn as her mom, obviously. But it wasn't her stubbornness so much as the continual distrust flickering behind her gaze that gnawed at Kip's spirit. Reaching for another box, he wondered if she saw that same look in his own eyes.

A thud followed by a burst of blue language snapped his head around. He spotted Sheridan halfway across the lawn, the box split open at her feet and groceries in a tumble all around her. A growl tore from her throat as she knelt to gather up the mess. Beau was already in the middle of it, his nose buried in a torn bag of tortilla chips.

"Beau, stop! You're fat enough already." Sheridan tried in vain to shove the dog aside.

Kip froze. Should he offer a hand and risk being snubbed again? Then he heard her sniffle, and the next thing he knew, he was on his knees beside her. He gave the dog a quick five-fingered poke in the ribs. "No! Sit!"

Beau obeyed instantly.

Sheridan swiped a hand across her cheek. "How'd you do that?"

"Just reminded him who was boss." Kip winked as he

gathered up canned goods and packaged foods. He tucked as much as he could into the crook of each arm and deposited the items on the top porch step, then went back for more.

By then, Sheridan had pulled herself together. She shot him an embarrassed smirk, though mist still clouded her eyes. "Guess I'm a little stressed out lately. I promise I don't usually cuss like a sailor."

"Believe me, I've heard a whole lot worse." Kip picked up a bag of brown rice and inspected the cellophane for any tears. It looked intact. Unlike his equilibrium just now. What was it about pretty women with tears in their eyes? Even stubborn ones like Sheridan Cross?

The back door slammed, and Mrs. Cross hurried down the porch steps. "Sheridan, don't tell me you tried to lift that big box all by yourself?"

"Don't rub it in, Mother." Clutching the torn chip bag in one hand and a can of mandarin oranges in the other, she pushed up from the grass. She sidestepped Kip, her eyes lowered. "I can get the rest. Thanks."

The last word sounded forced, like it pained her to admit she needed anyone's help.

No, make that Kip's help. Wasn't Tom Jacobs's approval good enough for her?

Kip shook off his questions and fetched a couple more boxes from the Tahoe before returning to the cottage.

He'd cleared out the kitchen area and was gearing up for some serious scouring when a knock sounded on the screen door. His hands dripping with soapy water, he ran a sponge down the front of a grimy cupboard. "It's open."

He took a few more swipes, and then the tapping grew louder. "It's open, I said. Come on in." About that time, another three raps rattled the screen. Shaking off the soap suds, he snatched a paper towel and dried his hands. "Hold your horses. I'm coming."

Weaving around trash bags and a jumble of mismatched furniture, Kip glimpsed Sheridan's back through the screen door. She shifted from foot to foot, looking as nervous as a cat on hot cement. When he said her name, she startled and whirled around.

Man, she was jumpy! Kip stepped through the door and pried a smile into his words. "Didn't you hear me answer?"

"I—yes, but—" Sheridan tucked her hands into her back pockets. "Mom said you should join us for supper. We'll eat in about an hour."

She retreated so fast that he never had the chance to reply, much less thank her for the offer.

Guess he'd be dining with the Cross ladies again tonight.

Mom must have known how hard it would be for Sheridan to walk up to that door and knock. Sheridan hadn't set foot in the little house in years, at least for anything that took longer than retrieving a box of Christmas decorations or tossing in a bag of used clothing destined for Goodwill. Did the house still reek of Ernie Finston's cigarette smoke? Would the kitchen still carry the aroma of Dell's homemade peanut butter cookies?

Sheridan didn't care if she never tasted another peanut butter cookie as long as she lived.

Not ready to face her conniving mother quite yet, Sheridan made a sudden detour into the barn. She paused in the square of sunlight just inside the door and gave her eyes a moment to adjust. Most of the horses were out in the pastures this time of day, but at the far end a quivering gray muzzle stretched over the stall door to sniff the air. A soft whicker called Sheridan closer.

"Hey, Gem." She let the gelding smell her palm. "Don't worry, you won't be stuck in the barn forever. We'll find you some friendly pasture mates soon, maybe a mare or two to flirt with. How's that sound?"

"Sounds mighty nice."

Sheridan swung around at the sound of the slow Texas drawl. The cowboy stood less than ten feet away, his face in shadows. Feeling like a kid caught peeking at Christmas presents, she sidestepped away from the stall and crossed her arms. "I didn't hear you."

"Came to check on Gem before I get cleaned up." Kip sidled past Sheridan to stroke the gray's neck. The horse responded with half-lidded eyes and pressed his face into Kip's chest.

The affection between man and horse brought a catch to Sheridan's throat. She edged nearer and ran her hand along the other side of the horse's neck. Gem graced her with a soft snuffle against her arm. The tickle of his whiskers made her giggle.

Kip laughed too. "I think he likes you."

Her eyes met his, and a tremor rippled through her belly. The cowboy looked different in this light. Less like a stranger. Less threatening. Less like a man she couldn't trust. She glanced away and whispered to Gem, "I think I like him too."

Chapter Four

Between bringing Nathan home from the hospital and getting things ready for Saturday's volunteer training, Sheridan didn't see Kip much over the next two days. But she quickly surmised he was every bit the horseman his references promised. He'd already analyzed the pasture groupings and immediately picked up on the fact that Belle, a bay mare with dominant tendencies, had grown a little too bossy with her pasture mates, particularly a gentle chestnut Arab named Lady. After some temperament assessment, Kip moved Lady in with a more compatible group of mares, and Belle found her new pasture mates not so easily intimidated.

At 5:45 Saturday morning, Sheridan's phone alarm roused her with an escalating chime. She sat up and stretched, then nearly tripped over Xena, who snored softly on her cushion. With a grunt, the dog rolled onto her back, her gangly legs pawing the air above her belly.

"Lazy dog." Sheridan scratched Xena's tummy and shuffled to the window. Behind the barn, the sun peeked an orange-gold eye above the treeline that ran along a stream.

Manuelo trundled a wheelbarrow full of manure and soiled shavings down the lane to the collection bin. The geldings had already been turned out in their pastures.

When Kip emerged through the barn door, Sheridan sucked in a tiny breath and edged back from the window. He led Belle and a palomino mare named Gigi along the lane toward pasture two, and Sheridan noted how politely each horse passed through the gate and stood quietly while Kip unlatched their halters.

Of course, five seconds later Belle was kicking up her heels in a morning dance clearly meant to remind everyone —Kip included—that she remained queen of this pasture.

Laughing to herself, Sheridan dressed for the day in jeans, a blue-and-yellow CROSS ROADS FARM T-shirt, and paddock boots. Time to help Mom get ready for the arrival of the sixteen prospective volunteers who'd signed up for training.

Passing the guest room downstairs, she heard Nathan's voice beyond the closed door. "Watch the arm."

A huff, then Kip's rough reply. "Not exactly my area of expertise. You good for now?"

"A cup of coffee would be nice."

The doorknob twisted, and Sheridan hurried on to the kitchen. She grabbed a glass from the cupboard and poured herself some orange juice as Kip ambled in. With a pasted-on smile, she leaned against the fridge and hoped he wouldn't notice her breathlessness. "How's Nathan this morning?"

"Fine. Coffee ready?" He crossed to the mug rack.

"Help yourself." Maybe the guy should learn sign language. Then he wouldn't have to talk at all. "You planning to join us for the volunteer training?"

"I'll be around." Kip filled two mugs, the rich aroma

permeating the kitchen. "Nathan asked if I'd work with Jet later, make sure he's okay after that tumble they took."

"I hope you'll be careful. Jet can be a handful." Although Sheridan guessed the cowboy had yet to meet the horse he couldn't handle.

The click of toenails announced Xena's entrance. Nose in the air, she headed straight for the island, where Mom had set out a tray of sweet rolls to serve the volunteers.

"Xena, no!" Sheridan rushed over, but not in time to keep the big dog from rearing up to rest both front paws on the island.

Just as Xena lunged to snatch a roll, Kip snapped his fingers and pointed to the floor. Meekly, the dog dropped onto all fours and cast Kip a repentant look, rolling her eyes until the whites showed along her lower lids.

Sheridan mashed her lips together. "Horses, dogs—is there any living creature you can't tame?"

Kip met her gaze for the briefest of moments before returning to the counter for the two mugs of coffee he'd poured. He muttered something under his breath that Sheridan couldn't make out at first, but as he started down the hall toward Nathan's room, she realized what he'd said: "*Myself.*"

Kip propped one foot on the fence rail outside the covered arena, where fifteen or twenty people sat on the bleachers at one end. Standing in front of them, Mrs. Cross and two other women took turns describing the history behind Cross Roads Farm and the equine therapy services they provided for at-risk, emotionally troubled, and physically or mentally challenged kids. Hearing it firsthand left Kip even more impressed.

Horses' hooves clip-clopped behind him, and he turned to see Sheridan leading Lady toward the arena entrance. Opening the gate for her, he asked, "Need a hand?"

"You could bring in Radar from pasture three. We need a couple of horses for a demonstration."

"On it."

Within minutes, Kip had fetched the sorrel quarter horse. Mrs. Cross took the lead rope and turned toward the bleachers. "This is our new barn manager, Kip Lorimer. You'll be seeing a lot more of him in the weeks ahead, so be sure to introduce yourselves."

Barn manager. So now he had a title. And it sounded a lot more permanent than what he'd had in mind. He watched the volunteer training awhile longer, and then decided he'd better get busy with Nathan's horse so he could finish up by noon. Later he needed to pick up a few groceries to stock his kitchen. Best to have a ready excuse in case the Crosses decided to invite him to a meal again. Spending too much time in the presence of Sheridan Cross was only asking for trouble.

Jet had a pasture to himself behind the smaller barn where he was stabled. Sleek and dark and full of himself, the spirited Warmblood pranced the perimeter of his domain like a young prince. Halter in hand, Kip unlatched the pasture gate and eased through. The horse trotted over, ears pricked forward, nostrils quivering.

"Hey, boy, lookin' mighty fine this morning." Kip stroked the horse's shoulder and draped the lead rope around his neck before slipping on the halter. The horse tried to pull away, but the looped lead rope gave Kip the advantage. After a couple of false starts, Jet snorted and allowed Kip to fasten the halter. With a pat on the neck, Kip led him through the gate.

Yes, indeed, this fella needed to burn off a whole lot of energy before Kip attempted a training ride. He released the horse into the round pen, took the longe whip from the hook, and stepped to the center. With a quick flick at the ground behind Jet's heels, Kip started the horse trotting around the circle at a lively pace.

After several reverses and gait changes, Jet began to drop his head and work his mouth. His ears cocked inward, the circle shrank slightly, and Kip could tell the horse was ready to "join up"—to accept Kip's leadership and partner with him. Kip dropped the whip, broke eye contact, and slowly turned away. He wiggled the fingers of his right hand, and within seconds Jet came up beside him and nuzzled his shoulder.

Only at the soft smattering of applause did Kip realize he had an audience. The volunteers and trainees had gathered around the rail, and their amazed looks suggested most of them had never seen the joining-up process before.

"That was beautiful." Sheridan edged through the gate and handed Kip Jet's halter. "I wish Nathan had seen this."

With a hesitant smile, Kip turned away to fasten the halter. The buckle felt slippery beneath fingers suddenly damp with perspiration. Sheridan's praise did something to his insides, made him want to stand up taller. His chin dipped slightly. His breath quivered out almost like Jet's a moment ago. If a human could cock an ear, Kip's would be aimed right at Sheridan Cross.

Sheridan pushed damp bangs off her forehead. *What just happened here?* A round pen demonstration, yes.

And a whole lot more.

She opened the gate, and the crowd parted for Kip to lead Jet out of the round pen. As he started for the barn, Mom directed the volunteers back to the arena. Sheridan sucked in a quick breath and detoured to the barn.

By the time she reached the door, whatever crazy emotions had propelled her this far had morphed into raging uncertainty. On the threshold, she seesawed on her heels—go inside, or march back to the arena before Kip noticed her presence?

He emerged from the tack room with a grooming tote. "Need something?"

Too late. Scrounging around in her brain for a good excuse, Sheridan strode forward to where Kip had secured Jet in the aisle with cross ties. "Though you might need to know which tack Nathan uses for Jet."

"He told me earlier. The Passier jumping saddle." Kip selected a rubber curry and set to work on Jet's neck and shoulder. "I'm good here if you need to get back to the training."

"It's covered. They'll be breaking for lunch soon anyway." She grabbed another curry and began working on Jet's other side, the circular motions bringing up loose hair and dust. "So you ride English, too? I pegged you as one hundred percent cowboy."

"Western's my preference, but I've done both." Kip briefly caught her eye over Jet's withers. For half a second the corner of his mouth lifted, and then his face disappeared behind the horse. "Variety is the spice of life, so they say."

Variety. Like moving from Texas to North Carolina?

Their eyes met once again as they reached Jet's tail. They finished off the horse's rump and hind legs, then traded the curries for stiff brushes. The rhythm of working in tandem felt good, right somehow. Sheridan didn't even mind the cowboy's typical silence.

Once again, they met at the horse's tail. Kip stowed away the brushes and found a hoof pick, and Sheridan stood at one side to watch. While he cleaned out the first hoof, something stirred in Sheridan's memory. "What did you mean when we were talking in the kitchen this morning?"

Kip steadied the horse's bent leg against his thigh. "About what?"

"I asked if there was any animal you couldn't tame. And I think you said yourself."

A harsh sigh and a forced laugh. Kip set Jet's left front foot down and moved to the rear leg. "Yeah, well . . . as you can see, I'm a little rough around the edges."

"I sure didn't see any rough edges when you were working Jet in the round pen."

Kip flicked a chunk of caked dirt out of Jet's hoof. "That's different."

"Different how?" Sheridan followed him around to the right hind foot and squared off in front of him.

He finished scraping out the hoof, then straightened and eased his back. "Hadn't you ought to go see if you can help your mom?"

"I'm just trying to learn a little more about you—especially since it looks like you're going to be working here for the foreseeable future. Is that a problem?"

"Yep." He backed up two steps and lifted Jet's right front hoof onto his thigh.

Sheridan marched two steps forward and crossed her

arms. "Yep? *Yep?* You drive all the way from Texas *just* to donate a horse to our program, and my mom offers you a job based on *one* reference from a stranger back in Texas, and that's all you can say?"

Kip scraped out the hoof and then stood, one hand resting on Jet's withers. "I'm just trying to do the job I was hired for. Either you believe I'm qualified or you don't. Now, which is it?"

Sheridan shrank beneath his sharp stare. She hadn't meant to offend him. In fact, she could scarcely believe how quickly he'd worked his way under her skin with his affinity for animals, his soft-spoken nature . . . and that entrancing Texas drawl.

Hands raised, she shuffled a half-step back. "I'm sorry. Sometimes my suspicion of strangers gets the best of me."

"I noticed." Kip headed into the tack room with the grooming tote.

Sheridan traipsed after him. "I have my reasons," she said, pausing in the doorway.

He hefted the jumping saddle off the rack and faced her. His expression softened slightly, and he closed his eyes for a moment. He hauled in a long, slow breath. "No need to explain. Excuse me. I've got a horse to ride."

As he brushed past her, Sheridan wished she could tame the wildness in her own heart—the part of her that wished Kip Lorimer had never driven his pickup onto Cross Roads Farm.

And the part of her that wished he'd never leave.

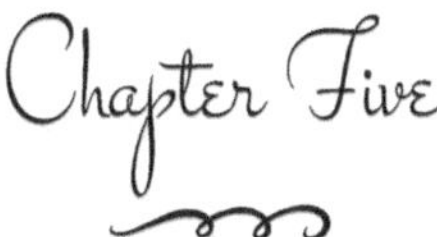

Chapter Five

On Tuesday morning at ten o'clock, a small yellow school bus rumbled up the driveway. Coming out of the barn, Kip coughed as dust drifted toward him on the light southerly breeze. This first class would include six foster kids from a group home, all with disciplinary problems. Several volunteers had already arrived, and Kip had been stocking six plastic pails with grooming tools.

A husky kid in a black T-shirt exited the bus first. The boy's you-can't-teach-me-anything attitude brought a frown to Kip's face. Yep, been there, done that.

"Slow down, Ryan." A beefy guy with a crew cut loped down the bus steps and snagged the boy's elbow. "Mind your manners, okay?"

Mrs. Cross came around the front of the bus. "Good morning, Dave. Right on time."

With a sharp glance clearly meant as a warning, the big man released the boy. "You're gonna have your hands full with this bunch, Linda."

"I'm sure we'll get along fine." Mrs. Cross nodded at Ryan with a warm smile, the same one she'd bestowed on

Kip at their first meeting. For maybe the space of a horse's whisker, the boy's mask of toughness eased. But by the time the next three kids bounded off the bus, his glare was back in place.

Two volunteers joined Mrs. Cross in escorting the kids to the arena as Sheridan strode over. "Hi, Kip. The horses ready?"

"In their stalls waiting. You want them in the arena now?"

"No, we'll send a volunteer along with each kid to get their own horse. It's part of the bonding process." She turned to go, then shot a grin over her shoulder, her blue eyes sparkling. "I saw that doubtful look in your eye as the kids got off the bus. Can't wait to see your expression eight weeks from now."

It wasn't doubt she'd read in his face. It was recognition. He didn't question for a minute the power of a horse to change a person. Horses sure had changed him. If Sheridan and her mom had known Kip when he was Ryan's age, they'd never have given him a chance.

On second thought, he felt pretty sure Mrs. Cross would have given him every chance in the world.

With a heavy sigh, he adjusted his Stetson and returned to the barn, where Manuelo was trundling a hay cart from stall to stall. Kip never tired of the barn sounds—the rustle of fresh shavings, horses munching on hay or snorting into their water pails.

"This will be a good day for *los niños*," Manuelo said with a grin. "*Dios es muy bueno.*"

God is very good? If God really cared, He'd have spared Kip from having to pull up stakes yet again to avoid another confrontation with the woman who'd long ago destroyed his trust and now couldn't seem to leave him in peace.

Manuelo wheeled the hay cart into the feed room, then paused to take a long swig from his water bottle. "You are worried about something, *Señor* Kip?"

"Just thinking." Kip ambled over to Gem's stall. The gray nickered and lifted his head over the gate to accept Kip's face rub. Today would be Gem's first day as a therapy horse. They'd been here barely a week, and Kip could honestly say he'd never seen the old boy looking more content. "You are one lucky fella, you know it?"

"Is not luck," Manuelo observed, coming up beside Kip. "God brought you here. Cross Roads Farm is a place of healing."

Kip buried his nose in the warm spot behind Gem's ear and inhaled. Musky horse scent permeated his brain like an elixir. An ache formed in his chest, like an emptiness longing to be filled. Could it really have been God who'd brought them here? Could there possibly be some higher purpose behind Kip's learning about Cross Roads Farm exactly when he'd needed a reason to leave Texas?

Sheridan sat on the porch swing and gazed out at the farm in the gathering dusk. The air smelled of rain, and distant lightning flashed against a backdrop of low clouds. It was Saturday already, and classes had gone well this week—first the kids from the group home, and then riding lessons for disadvantaged kids on Thursday. Saturdays were always the busiest, and this morning they'd held three separate sessions for kids with a variety of disabilities, including autism, cerebral palsy, and Down syndrome.

Sheridan was enjoying her time at the farm more than she expected. Though she visited Mom often, she always felt safer in Charlotte. She liked having friends and neighbors close by, and the police and fire department a quick 911 call away.

Exactly why she'd been so intent on getting Mom to sell the farm and move in with her.

But when she witnessed once again the joy in her mother's face as she worked with the volunteers or helped a kid like Ryan find just the right combination of gentle and firm as he learned to curry a horse, Sheridan knew Mom was in her element. And Mom was right—Cross Roads Farm was Dad's dream, ever since he'd inherited the farm from his own parents. Adopted at the age of eleven, Dad had once been a defiant troublemaker just like Ryan. But with patience, tenderness, and time with the horses, Dad had learned compassion and responsibility. More than that, he learned to love. It became his lifelong endeavor to bring that same healing to every child he could.

I miss you, Daddy. I miss you so much!

The clatter of a screen door drew Sheridan's attention to the caretaker's cottage. Kip stood on the tiny front stoop, thumbs tucked into the front pockets of his jeans. His hair looked damp, and he wore a clean white T-shirt, the smooth cotton clearly defining his taut muscles.

As he headed toward the barn, Sheridan noticed he was barefoot. Without his boots and the Stetson that too easily hid his features, he seemed more vulnerable. Her heart flip-flopped. Her hands tightened around the front edge of the swing.

"Sher?"

She jumped at the sound of Nathan's voice. The swing chains rattled.

"A little tense, are we?" Nathan plodded toward her and eased himself into a padded wicker chair.

"My mind was elsewhere, that's all."

"On a certain cowboy, if you ask me." Nathan attempted a nod toward the barn, but with the neck brace, the best he could manage was a pointed shift of his gaze.

Sheridan ignored him. Another lightning flash lit up the western sky, and several seconds later thunder rumbled. "I think a storm is coming."

"I think you're changing the subject."

Lucky guess. "If it rains too hard, we'll have to take the long way into town in the morning."

"So we'll have to get up twenty minutes earlier." Nathan yawned. "I'd sleep in if I could get away with it—not quite ready for a hard church pew—but since tomorrow's Father's Day, we should be there for Mom."

"Right, how could I forget?" Memories squeezed Sheridan's heart. "At least you seem to be getting around better."

"The pain meds help. Make my brain a little fuzzy, though."

Sheridan huffed a one-note laugh. "You mean fuzzier than normal."

"Not so fuzzy that I can't see what's going on between my sister and our resident cowboy."

Sheridan sprang from the swing so fast that it bounced back and caught her behind the thighs. "There is *nothing* going on between me and Kip Lorimer."

"Riiiight. I've been watching you two all week. Your eyes get all soft when you're around him. And I've seen how his eyes follow you when you don't know he's looking."

Sheridan stifled an unexpected frisson of pleasure. She crossed her arms and propped a hip against the porch rail. "You haven't set foot off this porch since you've been home. How can you possibly have made those observations?"

"You forget Kip comes over two or three times a day to give me a hand. Plenty close enough to watch you two making nice with each other."

"Nathan!"

Her sharp cry brought Beau and Xena bounding around from the side yard. Beau pushed his head under Nathan's hand, begging to be petted.

Nathan grimaced. "Easy, boy, or I'll have to go back inside."

"Maybe you should," she suggested, as much to avoid the dogs' roughhousing as to keep her brother from inventing more craziness about her and Kip.

A deafening crash of thunder sent Xena hurtling into Sheridan's legs with a whimper. She soothed the dog with gentle strokes while moving them both away from the porch rail. "It's okay, girl. Man, that was close!"

"No kidding." Nathan pushed up from the chair and shuffled toward the back door, Beau right beside him. "I think we'll all be safer inside."

"You and the dogs go ahead. I'll check on the horses."

"The horses. Right." Nathan shot her a crooked grin then turned serious. "Warn Kip about how Jet gets when it storms, okay?"

A nervous twinge shimmied up Sheridan's spine. Memories of other storms and Jet's volatile reactions made her hurry to shove her feet into the flip-flops she'd kicked off earlier. She dashed down the porch steps as the first drops of rain splattered the ground. Halfway across the yard, she heard the panicked thump of hooves against wood —not from the main barn, but from Jet's barn out back. The horse's anxious neighs cut through the night. She pictured Kip in his bare feet and prayed he kept his distance.

Hurrying through the main barn, she looked in on each horse and muttered a soothing word or offered a reassuring pat. Suddenly the sound of splintering wood and a man's shout made Sheridan spin around so fast that she careened against a stall. Gasping, she looked up as a black mass sped past her and out to the lane.

"Oh, no! Jet!"

Fool cowboy. How stupid could he be, going out to the barn without his boots? He'd only thought to look in on Gem once more, offer him a carrot or two. Then the storm came up out of nowhere and Jet freaked out. By the time Kip got to him, the horse's panic was out of control.

Sputtering choice words, Kip ignored the pain slicing through his right foot and limped after the fleeing horse. At the rate Jet exploded from his stall, he was probably out the front gate by now.

In the moments it took to cross the short space between the small and large barns, Kip was drenched by the downpour. He scraped the water out of his eyes and tried to think what to do next.

Then he noticed Sheridan coming toward him down the barn aisle, her short hair plastered against her skull and her clothes nearly as wet as his. They spoke at the same time.

"What are you doing out here?" Kip cried.

"You're limping," Sheridan said with a gasp. "Are you hurt?"

"It's nothing. A sliver in my foot, that's all." He noticed Sheridan rubbing her shoulder. "Did Jet—"

"No, no, just a bump." She grabbed his elbow and made him sit on a hay bale. "Here, let me see your foot."

Her cool, damp hands against his skin made him suck in his breath. He tried to pull his foot away, but she held fast to his ankle. He shuddered. "I should look for Jet before he hurts himself."

"We usually find him in one of the pastures after a storm. Hold still, will you?"

"Ow! Are you sure he won't go out to the road?"

"Not with the cattle guard."

Her fingers traced along the arch of his foot, sending shivers up his spine. He held his breath and tried not to flinch. "He could jump it."

"He won't. He just has to run off his panic until he settles down—there! It's out." Sheridan held up an inch-long sliver of wood. "Have you had a tetanus shot lately?"

Kip whistled between his teeth. "I'm good."

She frowned at him. "You don't look so good."

His foot felt fine. It was the rest of him he wasn't so sure about.

Letting a woman get this close? This wasn't good. Not good at all. He'd already made up his mind to be out of here by summer's end, staying only long enough to help with this round of therapy classes. Nathan would be better by then, or they could hire someone else.

The patter of footsteps drew his attention to the door. Mrs. Cross stepped inside and shook out an umbrella. "Everything okay in here?"

Sheridan stood abruptly and wiped her hands against the sides of her shorts. "I—we—Kip had a splinter in his foot."

"Oh, I see." Her lazy smile suggested maybe she saw a lot more. "I saw Jet race by the window. I think he ran into pasture four." She made a *tsk-tsk* sound. "Silly animal. Always thinks someplace else is safer than right where he is."

Kip knew that feeling. He pushed to his feet. "Sounds like the rain's stopping. I'd better get my boots on and bring him back to the barn."

Chapter Six

Knowing Kip sat just on the other side of Nathan in the church pew, Sheridan could barely concentrate. Hard enough missing Dad so much on Father's Day. Maybe having the cowboy along to distract them wasn't such a bad thing. Truth be told, Kip had surprised Sheridan when he finally accepted Mom's invitation. Clearly it had been awhile since he'd stepped inside a church. He fumbled with the hymnal pages and never seemed quite certain about when to stand or sit.

Yet even though Sheridan's faith still wavered at times, Kingsley's small community church remained a source of comfort. Their kindhearted pastor, Alan Wolfe, had spent many hours counseling her after that terrifying weekend so many years ago.

Not going there. She boxed up the memory and tucked it away once more in the recesses of her mind. Mom and Nathan were right—it was time to stop being so suspicious of every stranger who came into their lives. Kip was turning out okay, after all. A hard worker, reliable, skilled with horses.

And so easy on the eyes!

She could no longer deny her growing attraction to the quiet cowboy. She loved watching Kip at work, taking Jet through his paces in the jumping arena, exercising one of the therapy horses on a longe line, hefting a hay bale, or hosing off a sweaty horse in the wash stall.

And the feel of his bare foot in her hand as she'd plucked out the splinter—goose bumps ran up her arms just thinking about it.

"Sher." Nathan nudged her arm. "Sher, the hymnal."

"Sorry." The closing hymn already? Rising, she found the page and held the book to share with her brother—and hoped her face wasn't as red as it felt.

As they walked out to Mom's Tahoe after the service, Nathan claimed the front passenger seat. "Smoother ride," he said. "Easier on my neck."

"If you say so." Sheridan felt pretty sure that fake twitch in her brother's eye was really a self-satisfied wink.

Mom climbed in behind the steering wheel. "Anybody up for lunch at Kingsley Station?"

Nathan held up his casted left arm and wiggled his fingers. "I might need a little help with my burger."

"I'd be delighted to assist." Maybe if Sheridan kept her brother's mouth full, he couldn't tease her anymore about Kip.

Go out for lunch? Kip was still processing his feelings about being in church again, but after Manuelo's suggestion that God had purposely brought Kip and Gem to Cross Roads Farm, he thought maybe he should give church another try.

Or was it really because he couldn't resist spending

Sunday morning in the company of the amazingly beautiful Sheridan Cross? Remembering last night, her gentle fingers stroking the sole of his foot in search of the sliver . . . it was a good thing he had his hat to hold on to just now because his hands started to tremble all over again.

The Kingsley Station restaurant hostess seated them in a round booth overlooking train tracks behind the building, which once must have been a train depot. Nathan somehow finagled it so Kip and Sheridan took the inside seats, between him and Mrs. Cross. When their server brought the oversized menus, Kip couldn't turn pages without bumping elbows with Sheridan.

Not that it mattered, because with all his senses attuned to the woman at his left, Kip might as well have been reading hieroglyphics.

After the server took their orders, Mrs. Cross sipped her water, then sat back with a sigh. "It's been a good first week of summer classes."

"Dad would be proud." Nathan's voice held no trace of his usual teasing tone. Eyes misty, he lowered his head. "Our first Father's Day without him. Didn't know it would be so hard."

Sheridan unfolded her napkin and spread it on her lap. "I like to believe he's watching from heaven."

"Me, too, sweetie." Mrs. Cross turned to Kip. "I wish you could have met my husband. You two would have gotten along famously."

Kip could only nod as memories of his own father crowded in. Sometimes he missed Dad so badly that it hurt. If not for the mentors who'd taken Kip under their wing after his dad died, he'd surely have ended up a messed-up kid in a group home just like that Ryan boy.

"We'd love to hear more about your family, Kip." Mrs.

Cross tore open a package of crackers. "Are your parents still in Texas?"

"Yes, ma'am." His mom, anyway. And he hoped she stayed there.

"Any brothers or sisters?"

"Only child." Which was probably a good thing, considering.

The arrival of their food saved him from further explanations. The savory aroma of buffalo burger on a toasted wheat bun had him thinking of nothing more urgent than satisfying his rumbling stomach.

By the time Nathan polished off most of his burger with a messy, one-fisted grip, he'd teased Sheridan into resuming their usual brother-sister banter. Mrs. Cross took turns laughing at their silliness or scolding them for picking on each other.

Kip couldn't help chuckling over the brother-sister act. He nudged Mrs. Cross. "Have these two always been like this?"

She answered with an exaggerated eye roll. "This is *nothing* compared to how they were growing up! At least they finally outgrew the urge to strangle each other."

"Don't count on it!" Sheridan tossed a piece of lettuce at her brother.

He came right back at her with a soggy mushroom. "Wait till I'm out of this neck brace and have two good hands again."

"Kids!" Mrs. Cross tapped the table with her knuckles, but a bubble of laughter took some of the bite out of her stern glare.

Sheridan bumped Kip with her shoulder. "If you'd like a brother, I know where you can get one—cheap!"

"You got one for sale?" Kip grinned. He'd gladly take the fun-loving Nathan as a brother any day.

On the other hand, having Sheridan as a sister was the *last* thing he wanted.

In fact, if she worked her way much deeper into his heart, he might find it next to impossible to ever leave Cross Roads Farm.

"Rats." Sheridan set her cell phone on the counter and tore her fingers through her hair. Just when she had her summer all planned out.

Mom turned from stirring penne pasta into a skillet meal she was preparing for their Monday evening supper. "Who was on the phone?"

"My principal, Mrs. Ingram. There's a special two-week teacher enrichment class at UNC Charlotte she really wants me to take. The first class was today."

"And she's just now telling you about it?"

Sheridan set plates around the table. "The upper elementary special-ed teacher just found out she's pregnant with twins and doesn't plan to return in the fall. Mrs. Ingram wants to move me up from K-2, and this course is specifically tailored for the needs of that age group."

"So . . . kind of a good news/bad news thing." Mom snipped some fresh basil off the plant in the windowsill and stirred it into the pasta and veggies.

"I've always wanted to work with the older kids, so it's a great opportunity." Sheridan finished arranging flatware and napkins, then laid her chin on her mother's shoulder. "But I hate leaving you in the lurch."

Mom patted Sheridan's cheek. "This is your career

we're talking about. And we've got plenty of volunteers this summer, not to mention what a great job Kip's doing."

"He's pretty cool, isn't he?" Sheridan went to fill glasses with iced tea.

"Hmm, I think you're *really* concerned about spending two weeks away from our handsome cowboy."

Nathan strolled into the kitchen just then. "Handsome cowboy? I know for sure you aren't talking about *me*!"

Faking a growl, Sheridan carried the tea glasses to the table. "Honestly, you two!"

"Only three place settings? Couldn't talk the 'handsome cowboy' into joining us?"

Sheridan resisted the urge to punch her invalid brother in the arm. "Didn't ask. He looked a little shell-shocked by the time we got home from church yesterday."

Not to mention she hadn't seen much of Kip at all today. After exercising a few of the horses early this morning, he'd disappeared into the barn and had hardly shown his face since.

"He's doing something in the tack room." Mom set a trivet in the center of the table. "Said it was a surprise."

"Seriously?" Sheridan ambled over to the window. "Did he say anything to you, Nathan?"

"Are you kidding? That guy is about as talkative as a rock." Nathan eased into a chair. "Why don't you go ask him yourself? Flutter your baby blues. He'll be putty in your hands."

Sheridan whirled around and stopped herself just short of bopping her brother on the head. "Brother mine, you aren't the only one who can't wait until you're out of that neck brace."

"Let's eat, kids." Mom brought the skillet to the table and pulled out a chair. "And, Sher, it's unanimous. After supper you're elected to find out what our resident cowboy is up to."

"Since when do I not get a vote?" Not that she wasn't equally curious about what had kept Kip busy all day. And Mom was right—she really would miss their daily encounters as he worked with the horses and helped with the therapy classes.

Was she crazy for letting this attraction to a virtual stranger grow so quickly? Honestly, what did they *really* know about the man? So Kip was good-looking.

Ernie Finston was a regular Rhett Butler, and Dell could ignite a bonfire with that gorgeous mane of red hair.

So Kip was good with horses.

Ernie Finston ran the barn like a general overseeing his troops.

So Kip was charming.

The Finstons were charming—charmed their way right into the Crosses' good graces and then cleaned them out.

The last few bites of Sheridan's supper hit the bottom of her stomach like a brick. Kip was holed up in the tack room, huh? Right along with several thousand dollars' worth of saddles, bridles, and other gear. Would they wake up in the morning to find him—and all their tack and maybe a horse or two—long gone?

She laid down her fork. "Excuse me. I think I'll go check on that cowboy now."

And maybe she'd find Dad's old squirrel rifle and take it along—just for show, of course.

Because no way would she allow another charming stranger to ruin their lives.

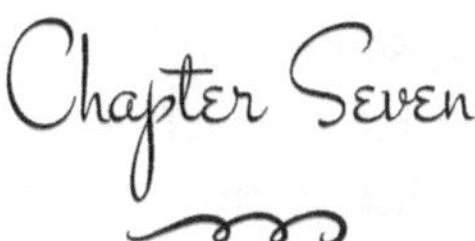

Chapter Seven

Kip sat on a wooden bench, his saddle-making tools scattered around him and the scent of leather and saddle soap thick in the air. While helping with the equine therapy classes, he'd noticed several pieces of tack needed cleaning and repair. Since he had the necessary tools and skills, he could save Mrs. Cross the expense.

He laughed to himself at the look on Mrs. Cross's face when she'd asked him what he was up to. He'd simply responded, "Consider it a thank-you for yesterday's lunch in town."

Lunch and a whole lot more.

Was he finally mellowing? Was he ready at long last to let someone—a woman—into his life?

A woman like Sheridan Cross?

"Kip?" A sharp knock sounded outside the door. Sheridan burst into the room. "What exactly are you—oh!"

Kip froze, his left hand gripping the bridle he'd been mending. His mouth spread into a hesitant smile. "Hey."

"Hey, yourself." Whatever had been eating at Sheridan appeared to melt away like soap suds down the wash stall drain. She waved a hand in a gesture that took in the whole tack room. "*This* is what you've been doing all day? Cleaning tack?"

"Cleaning. Mending. Whatever needed doing." Kip resumed his work stitching up a frayed seam along the bridle's crown piece. "I meant it to be a surprise."

When Sheridan didn't answer, he glanced up to find those blue eyes boring a hole right through him. "I–I–I'm sorry, Kip. So sorry—" One hand flew to her mouth, and she made a small choking sound before backing out the door and tearing off in a run.

"Sheridan, wait!" Kip dropped the bridle and chased after her. He grabbed her wrist and spun her around, but at her startled cry, he quickly released his grip. A whole different emotion filled her face—fear, horror?

He slowed his breathing and stood quietly, eyes lowered, same as he did to calm a skittish horse. "Didn't mean to scare you." He longed to reach out and stroke that soft, pink cheek but kept his hands at his sides. "Did I do something wrong?"

A pained sigh whispered between Sheridan's lips. Her shoulders rose and fell, and she finally met his gaze. "No, Kip. You didn't do anything wrong. It's just me. Me and my foolish lack of trust."

Maybe it was Kip's ease with the horses and dogs. Maybe it was the fact that he didn't always jump in to fill dead air space in a conversation. His quietness alone invited her to talk—and he seemed to know Sheridan *needed* to talk, to force the ghosts of the past out into the open and finally face them down.

In the gathering dusk, they sat hip to hip on the arena bleachers. "I haven't been fair to you," she said, hands clasped between her knees. "I've thought the worst, just because you're a stranger." She gave a low chuckle. "Well, you *were* a stranger when you first pulled up in that rusty old pickup."

"You bad-mouthing my pickup?" Kip tipped back his cowboy hat and narrowed his eyes.

Sheridan laughed and yanked the hat right off his head. When he tried to snatch it back, she held it at arm's length. "I bet you even sleep in this dirty old thing."

"First my pickup, now my hat." Kip crossed his arms. "Can't a hardworking cowboy get any respect?"

His comment turned her serious once more. She sighed and handed him his hat. "I mean it, Kip. I really am sorry."

He fingered the hat brim for a moment and then laid it aside on the bleacher seat. "I could tell from the minute we met that you didn't trust me. Not that you had any reason to."

"No, but I didn't have any reason *not* to." A long, tired breath scraped through her chest. "It's just that since my dad died, I worry about my mom being alone out here. The day before you showed up, I was trying to convince her to sell the farm and move into Charlotte with me."

"It *is* a pretty big operation, a lot for a single woman to keep up with."

"Oh, Mom can keep up with it just fine. You've seen how strong she is, how organized, how—"

"Bossy?"

She angled Kip a knowing gaze. "I wasn't going to use that word, but since you did . . ."

"I meant it in only the most respectful way."

Sheridan smirked. "Mom would be the first to admit

it's true. She's always been the backbone of Cross Roads Farm, and now that Dad's gone, it means even more to her."

"Then why would you try to talk her into selling?"

Words caught in Sheridan's throat. An aching lump swelled behind her heart. "Because it's too easy for her to trust people like you."

His back stiffened. His blue-jeaned knee moved a fraction of an inch away from hers. "I get the picture."

"No, you don't. Not the whole picture." Sheridan rested her hand on his forearm, feeling the tautness of his muscle. She held firm until the tension ebbed and he gave her his eyes.

Such sadness in that shadowed stare! A depth of hurt that made her heart clench to think she'd put it there.

"Please believe me, Kip. It's not you."

He trapped her trembling fingers between his palms. "You've been about to tell me something ever since we came out here. What is it, Sher? Just say it."

His use of her nickname brought a shiver. That, and his closeness. Warmth radiated off his body, the man-smells filling her senses. His scent, though heavy with sweat from a day's work, somehow comforted and reassured her, while the acrid, fear-laced stench of Ernie Finston had made her retch.

And Dell's cookies, the peanut-butter cookies. Sheridan swallowed the bile that rose with the memory.

"I was twelve when it happened." The words clawed past the knot in her throat. "Daddy had taken Nathan on a Cub Scout camping trip. Mom and I were here alone. Us and the Finstons."

"The Finstons?"

"Ernie managed the horses. Dell, his wife, did some

cooking and cleaning for us. She also babysat sometimes when Mom and Dad needed to be away."

Kip nodded toward the caretaker's cottage. "They lived here on the farm?"

"For two years." Bitterness threatened to strangle her. "Two years of worming their way into our lives, earning my parents' trust, ingratiating themselves to Nathan and me like a favorite aunt and uncle—and all the while they were using the farm as home base while robbing houses all over the county."

The pressure of Kip's hands increased. "Yours, too?"

"Not that we knew of, until . . ." She told him then how Dell had invited her into the cottage to sample some freshly baked cookies. How Ernie had grabbed and held her while Dell slapped duct tape across her mouth, and then yanked her wrists behind her and bound them with more tape.

Then they'd tossed her onto the bed like a sack of grain. While Dell taped her ankles together, Ernie loomed close, the smell of him nearly choking her as he tied a rope around her waist and then lashed it to the bedstead. He told her to lie there like a good little girl or they'd kill her mother.

Sheridan brushed her tears away with an angry swipe. "I still had a piece of cookie in my mouth, and I couldn't even swallow it. I could hardly breathe through my own tears and saliva. All I could do was pray they wouldn't hurt Mom."

Kip's breath whispered across her temple. "You must have been scared out of your mind."

"I didn't know what they were doing, whether Mom was alive or dead or—" She pulled her hand from Kip's and clenched her fists, rocking on the bleacher seat until she was able to control her voice. "It was just getting dark when I finally heard the Finstons' voices outside the window. There was a lot of banging and cackling laughter. Then their pickup started up and roared away."

Kip found her hand again and gently massaged her knuckles. "Did they . . . did they hurt you? Or your mom?"

"No, not physically." If she didn't count the wrists and ankles rubbed raw and the throat swollen nearly shut from thirst and endless futile attempts to cry for help. "I found out later they'd surprised Mom in the house and locked her in a closet. Then they tore the house apart in search of anything of value, loaded it into their pickup and took off."

Kip muttered a curse. "How'd you finally get free?"

A ragged groan tore through Sheridan's chest. "There was nothing Mom or I could do until Dad and Nathan got home from the campout the next day."

Kip lifted Sheridan's hand to his lips then dropped his forehead against his fists. "It's no wonder you distrusted me."

The sun had long ago set behind the trees, and Kip's hunched form was a mere shadow against a purple-orange sliver of sky. Sheridan's heart broke for the cowboy who'd played no part in the trauma of her childhood yet who now bore the scars from her lack of trust. Gently she tugged her hand from his grasp and placed both palms against his face. "I was wrong, Kip. Please forgive me."

He wanted to kiss her so badly it hurt. Somewhere deep down in his belly a gnawing hunger raged, a yearning unlike anything he'd ever felt. Her hands against his face made him shudder—did she feel it? He swiveled on the seat, and her hands fell away. He forced himself to breathe past the pain, the wonderful, terrible, heart-searing pain ripping through his chest.

"I left a mess in the tack room," he said, pushing to his feet. He snatched up his hat and jammed it on his head.

"You didn't answer me."

He looked down at her. *What were we just talking about?*

"Please, Kip. I have to go back to Charlotte tomorrow, and I need to know you forgive me."

"I told you, I understand—" His head suddenly felt like a ping-pong ball. Or maybe it was his heart. "You're *leaving?*"

"I just found out I have to get back for a two-week class. I need it for my job." She stood next to him on the bleacher step, and he fought to keep his hands at his sides. "A week ago—actually, only an hour ago—I wouldn't have been able to leave with any sense of peace. Maybe Mom's faith is finally rubbing off on me, or maybe it's what I see in your face every time I look at you, but I know in my heart that you're a good person. I know you're trustworthy. I know you'd never hurt me or my family."

"I wouldn't—*couldn't.*" Kip stepped off the bleachers and took three long strides across the packed earth. He stopped and turned. "You're coming back, though? After the two weeks?"

Oh, mercy! Did he sound as desperate to her as he did to himself?

Gentle laughter floated toward him. "What, afraid you can't handle my mom and brother without me?"

"I—no, it's just—" Blithering idiot. He gave a helpless shrug. "I just wondered what your plans were."

She hopped to the ground, her sandals slapping the dirt. As she strode toward him, the glow from the yard light revealed a pearly grin. "Yes, I'll be back. And I plan to be here for the weekend to help with next Saturday's classes."

Kip couldn't seem to make his voice work, so he settled for a grin of his own. Two weeks at Cross Roads Farm and his sense of belonging was ten times what it had ever been in Nacogdoches or Big Spring or El Paso or Amarillo or anywhere else he'd tried to put down roots.

Dear God, don't let this feeling ever end.

Chapter Eight

"Well?" Mom eyed Sheridan over her laptop screen. "You were out there long enough. Did you find out what Kip's been doing all day?"

Sheridan leaned against the study doorway and crossed one ankle over the other. "He's been cleaning and mending our tack."

A disbelieving smile skewed Mom's lips. "That man."

Sheridan plopped into a barrel-shaped side chair. "He's just finishing up. He'll be in shortly to check on Nathan."

Mom tapped some computer keys and then closed the lid. "Kip truly is a godsend. The Lord must have known we'd need him this summer, what with Nathan's accident and now this class you'll be attending."

"How do you do it, Mom?"

"Do what, honey?"

"After all we've been through—the Finstons, losing Dad, the scare with Nathan—how do you keep your faith so strong?"

Mom spread her arms. "Come here, sweetie."

Kneeling at her mother's feet, Sheridan stretched her

arms around Mom's waist and nestled against her. "I love you, Mom."

"*This* is how I keep my faith strong. I know God loves me more deeply and profoundly than I could possibly love my own children—and that's a lot!"

Sheridan relished her mother's embrace in sweet silence, until a troubling thought niggled at her brain. She sat back on her heels. "Kip never talks about his own family. You've seen the look in his eyes anytime we've asked."

"I figure he'll tell us more when he's ready." Mom ran her fingers through Sheridan's hair. "And maybe that's another reason God sent him to us—to experience the closeness of a loving family like ours."

Sheridan laid her head on her mother's thigh. "I told him tonight about the Finstons. I told him it's why I couldn't trust him at first. And I apologized."

Mom's chair creaked. A soft, sibilant sigh slipped out. "That's good, sweetie. I'm glad you could finally talk about it with someone. I'm glad it was Kip."

"Me, too."

Kip watched Sheridan's red Prius drive away only minutes before the school bus arrived with the kids from the group home. When Mrs. Cross cornered him with some last-minute instructions, the hollowed-out feeling in the pit of his stomach made it hard to pay attention.

Letting a woman burrow so deep into his heart? *Definitely* not part of the plan.

Mrs. Cross tugged on his shirtsleeve. "Kip, are you listening? One of our volunteers is out sick. I need you in the arena."

"Uh, okay." Still not totally focused, he followed her through the gate.

The six kids from the home sat lined up on the bleachers—two girls, four boys, all in jeans and ratty T-shirts. Ryan, the surly kid from last week, slumped on the far end and stared across the fields.

When Mrs. Cross led Kip straight toward the boy, warning bells went off in his brain. "Hang on here. I thought you meant help with the horses."

"Trust me, it'll be okay." She hooked her elbow through Kip's and planted herself directly in Ryan's line of sight. "This is Kip. He'll be your barn buddy today. I thought you'd enjoy working with each other since Kip is the one who brought Gem to us."

"Yeah?" For a nanosecond Kip thought he saw admiration in the boy's eyes. Then Ryan's mouth flattened. "He's such a lousy horse that you gave him away, huh? Figures."

Kip bit his tongue before he told this kid where to get off. Even so, he couldn't stop his next words. "Nope. He's such a *great* horse that I figured he'd be just the thing to straighten out snotty kids like you."

Mrs. Cross winced, but she kept her friendly smile in place. "I'll leave you two to get acquainted. You can bring Gem in from the pasture, collect your pail of grooming tools, and get started." With a reassuring pat on Kip's shoulder, she marched away.

Man, oh man, what had he gotten himself into?

Ryan dropped one leg to the ground and stood. Not quite as tall as Kip, but with his broad chest and square jaw, he still made an imposing figure. He shot Kip a lazy grin. "Guess Ol' Lady Cross showed *you* who's boss."

Kip donned an easy grin of his own and moved in

closer, hands on hips. "*Mrs.* Cross *is* the boss, and you'll treat her and everyone else around here—including the horses—with respect."

The boy frowned but didn't say a word. Kip nodded toward the arena exit and led the way to the geldings' pasture.

"Hey, where're we going? The horses were in the barn last week."

"Only to make it easier for greenhorns like you. This week you get to fetch your own horse." He stopped at the gate, where four halters hung with lead ropes attached. "You know which halter is Gem's?"

"The one with his name on it, natch. You think I'm dense?" Ryan heaved a sigh worthy of an Oscar and reached for the royal blue halter and rope. Slinging it over his shoulder, he unlatched the gate and gave it a shove. He marched into the pasture, and immediately the four geldings took off running. "Hey! Stupid horses, get over here *now*!"

From Kip's perspective, it wasn't the horses who were stupid. "You like it when someone storms into your space with an attitude like that?"

Ryan snorted. "See, even the horses hate me."

"They don't hate you. They just don't trust you." Kip stepped quietly to the boy's side. "Since you walked in that gate, you've broken just about every rule of good horsemanship. Number one, this pasture is their home and you're a guest. So you don't invite yourself in without politely asking permission."

"Ask permission? How?"

"A kind word would be a good start."

"Like, 'Hey, Mr. Horse, can I come in?'"

"That works just fine. But watch your tone. Horses

aren't particularly fond of sarcasm." With a hand on Ryan's shoulder, Kip turned him back the way they'd come. "Rule number two. *Always* shut the gate behind you. A horse gets out and no telling where he'll end up. Maybe on the front grill of a semi."

"Ouch." Ryan latched the gate. "What's rule number three?"

Maybe they were getting somewhere. Kip glanced around and noticed Gem and a couple of the other geldings had come a little closer, watching with curious eyes. "Rule number three is to approach slowly and calmly, without making eye contact. Like this."

Kip chose an angled path toward Gem, humming softly as he walked. Nearing the horse's shoulder, he stretched one hand along Gem's neck with gentle but firm strokes. "A little closer," he told Ryan. "And turn your body sideways." Kip directed Ryan to Gem's side. "Now *gently* loop the lead rope around his neck. That gives you something to grab in case he decides he doesn't want to stick around."

"Hey, cool." This time not a hint of sarcasm laced the boy's words. "Now the halter?"

"Now the halter. Stay out of his face, though. Stand by his cheek and slip the halter up over his nose—that's it. Now take the lead rope and you're ready to go."

Gem nickered and rubbed his nose along Ryan's arm. "I think he likes me!"

Kip chuckled. "What's not to like?"

The grin lighting the boy's face did something to Kip's heart, not unlike the feeling he got when a horse joined up with him in the round pen. Communication. Understanding. Trust.

Yep, Kip could really learn to like it here at Cross Roads

Farm. He found himself wishing Sheridan had seen this—and realized he missed her more than ever.

The course was interesting, but Sheridan had an awful time keeping her focus. She missed Mom and Nathan. She missed Xena. But why not let the dog enjoy a summer vacation, too, instead of staying cooped up in the townhouse?

And she missed Kip Lorimer. Missed his smile, his lazy walk, his incredible confidence around the horses. And yes, she even missed that silly hat ring permanently etched into his sandy blond hair.

As she walked to her car after class Thursday evening, Greg Mason, one of the other teachers, matched her stride. "You free for dinner?"

Sheridan angled a glance his way and assumed one of her well-practiced brush-off smiles. She picked up her pace. "Sorry, I have plans."

Which basically involved heating up a frozen entrée. Besides, she'd only met the guy three days ago.

"I mean it, you haven't tasted Italian till you've eaten at Mauricio's." Greg's arm brushed hers, making her flinch.

"I've been there—not one of my favorites." Sheridan spied her Prius near the far end of the row. She'd make a run for it if she wouldn't look like a complete idiot.

"Somewhere else, then. You name the place."

Sheridan halted and gripped her leather portfolio in front of her like a shield. "I *said* I have plans."

He lifted a hand, palm outward. "I get it. You're not interested. Sorry I bothered you."

Greg turned and marched away. Sheridan couldn't say

she felt sorry to see him go, but guilt plagued her for treating him so coolly. He was just trying to be friendly—probably noticed she wasn't wearing a wedding ring and thought it wouldn't hurt to try.

Twenty minutes later, she pulled into the covered parking area next to her building, then carefully scanned her surroundings before starting toward her front door. She already regretted leaving Xena at the farm. At least the oversized lap dog provided a comforting presence, especially at night when the creepy sounds started up. Sheridan hadn't enjoyed a good night's sleep all week.

After eating her tasteless frozen entrée, she settled in on the sofa to read a class assignment, but struggled to keep her eyes open long enough to finish a page.

A *scritch-scritch* at the window snapped her awake. The textbook thudded to the floor. She tiptoed to the window and peeked through the drapes. A tree branch—good grief.

Her cell phone, still on vibrate, started dancing across the end table. She snatched it up and checked the Caller ID. "Hey, Mom."

"I haven't heard from you since you left for Charlotte. You okay?"

"Just peachy." Sheridan crossed one leg over the other. "I'd sure rather be there with you."

"Your class isn't interesting?"

"It's fine. It's just . . ." She flung an arm across her eyes. "Mom, am I completely hopeless?"

Her mother laughed in surprise. "Where did *that* come from?"

"One of the other teachers in my class—a pretty good-looking guy, actually—tried to get me to go out with him tonight. I wouldn't even give him the time of day."

"Oh, honey." Sheridan pictured her mother massaging

her forehead while she tried to figure out how to talk her daughter through yet another boyfriend crisis.

Make that *lack* of boyfriends. Throughout high school and college, when Sheridan's girlfriends gossiped about dates and proms and engagement parties and weddings, she remained perennially unattached. Not that boys ignored her—in fact, she regularly found herself pursued by some of the coolest guys on campus. Sure, the attention flattered her. But let a boy get close? They smelled. They hovered. They sweet-talked and complimented and wheedled in hopes of getting more than she was willing to give.

Blame it on Ernie Finston. No, he hadn't hurt her in *that way*. But he'd left her with a latent distrust of men in general.

"Honey, all men are not like Ernie Finston," Mom said as if reading her mind.

"I know, I know. All I have to do to believe that is remember Dad." Sheridan flicked a tear off her cheek.

Mom gave a low chuckle. "Believe me, your dad had his share of warts and weaknesses."

"Yes, but I always knew I could trust him."

"And you will find a man of your own someday who will love you just like your daddy loved me."

An image of Kip Lorimer rose in Sheridan's mind. "Mom?"

"Yes?"

"What if I've already met the guy?"

Chapter Nine

"Easy, boy." Kip massaged Jet's reins as they approached the jump, then gave him just enough head to sail effortlessly over the rails.

Man, this horse was a dream! Not the best mount for Nathan, though, judging from what Kip had gleaned about Nathan's on-again, off-again riding experience. Jet moved like a case of nitro ready to detonate. Kip wouldn't even get on the horse's back until after he'd worked him a good twenty minutes in the round pen.

Kip cantered the horse around the perimeter while he chose his next fence. One more and he'd call it a day. Besides, it was Friday, and Sheridan would be back by suppertime. Mrs. Cross had already invited him to join them. He'd need a shower first. And maybe another shave. Five o'clock had come and gone.

The Liverpool—Jet was finally getting over his resistance to the water jump, and another successful run would boost his confidence even more. Kip reined Jet toward the three-foot fence at the pond, and the horse adjusted his stride perfectly. All Kip had to do was ride him over.

A flash of red diverted his attention for a split second—just long enough for him to lose his seat and land in the water while Jet hit dry ground on the other side of the pond and cantered away.

Sheridan bolted from her car and scrambled over the fence rail. "Kip! Are you hurt?"

Humiliation soaked him down to his soggy boots. He pushed to his feet and stood in the ankle-deep pond. Yanking off his riding helmet, he muttered, "I'm fine."

Sheridan splashed into the pond, spattering her cropped pants with flecks of the muddied water. Her gaze combed every inch of him. Her hands fluttered as if she wanted to feel for any broken bones just to be sure.

He almost wished she would. Except then he'd probably end up doing the one thing he'd been longing to do since Monday—kiss the living daylights out of her.

He tossed the helmet into a clump of grass and reached for her hands to still them—and his own. "I mean it. I'm okay."

"After what happened to Nathan—what *could* have happened—at least you were wearing a helmet."

"I'm not stupid." Okay, so a lot of the time he was, as were most of the cowboys he knew. Wearing a helmet was for sissies. But in two short weeks, Mrs. Cross and the other volunteers had drilled into him the importance of safety first. Not to mention he'd quickly concluded that only a fool would attempt to ride Jet without a helmet.

Sheridan plucked a wet leaf off his shoulder. One corner of her mouth turned up. "I still can't get used to the sight of a cowboy riding English."

"Don't change the subject. It was your fault, you know." Kip sloshed out of the pond, pulling her along. "If you hadn't picked that moment to drive past in your flashy red car—"

"I thought the mark of a good horseman was being able to keep his seat amid all kinds of distractions."

If you only knew how you distract me! Kip bent down to retrieve his helmet. "Go on, get out of here. I'd better catch Jet before he trips on his reins." He noticed she wasn't moving. "What?"

She smirked. "I'll be happy to go as soon as you let go of my hand."

He looked down at her dainty fingers cradled in his grimy, callused fist. Warmth flooded up his arm, into his chest. His breathing grew shallow.

"Kip?" A dreamy look misted her eyes.

He inched closer. "Sher, I—"

Something thumped against his back. He stumbled against Sheridan and wrapped his arms around her to keep them both from tumbling to the ground. Her short curls brushed his cheek, and the apple scent of her shampoo sent his senses reeling. He squeezed his eyes shut and savored a moment of heaven.

A wet-sounding snort and the tickle of horse whiskers on his neck snapped him out of the reverie. He reluctantly released Sheridan and positioned himself between her and the horse. "Great timing, Jet."

Sheridan huffed. "That's a matter of opinion."

"Maybe he's smarter than we are." Kip gathered up Jet's dangling reins. "Go on, before this guy smashes one of those pretty painted toenails."

She backed slowly away. "See you later?"

"I'm not goin' anywhere."

The night air pulsed with the sounds of crickets, frogs, and the occasional hoot of an owl. Sheridan relished the serenity, noisy as it could be on a summer evening like this. Stars shimmered overhead, a thick blanket of sparkling lights. People living in the city would never believe the sky contained so many stars.

She sat on the front porch steps, Kip beside her, their hands intertwined. Moments ago Mom had poked her head out the door to say she'd be turning off the porch light. "So you can see the stars better," she said.

Right. And Mom had performed a masterful job of their suppertime seating arrangements, making sure Kip had no choice but to take the chair next to Sheridan's.

Did Kip have any clue he'd become the object of such scheming? If so, he hadn't let on. When he spoke at all, he talked about his work with Jet or one of the therapy horses. And goose bumps rose on Sheridan's arms when he told how he and Gem had begun to break through that belligerent boy Ryan's tough shell.

"Nice evening," Kip murmured beside her. "I could really learn to like it here."

"I'm glad." She heard the hopeful smile in her voice and quickly looked away. A petal from Mom's Perfect Moment rose bush lay on the step. Only one thing could make *this* moment more perfect. She stroked the petal between her thumb and forefinger, its fruity fragrance like a whisper in the air. "You think you might stay awhile?"

"I've thought about it." Kip ran his thumb along the back of her hand. He started to say more but seemed to catch himself. He rose and ambled across the lawn, then tipped his head back and let his gaze roam the night sky.

Sheridan joined him. "What are you looking for up there?"

"Answers."

"Finding any?"

He sighed and faced her. "Do you pray?"

"I try. Do you?"

"I think I'm just now learning how again. Not sure I'm hearing any answers, though."

Sheridan hooked her arm through his and rested her head against his shoulder. The knotted muscle provided a firm pillow beneath her cheek—solid and comforting all at the same time. "Can I ask what you're praying about?"

"Guess you have a right to know." Kip extracted his arm and then tenderly pulled her against him, tucking her head under his chin.

She slid her arms around his torso and snuggled into him. Nothing in her life had ever felt so right, so perfectly wonderful. His thudding heart against her ear said more than any words ever could. Still, she had to ask, hoping he'd say the words she longed to hear. "Well? Are you going to tell me or not?"

"I'm praying for the Lord to let me stay in one place long enough to make a real life for myself. Someplace where I can finally belong."

"Do you think maybe you've found that place?" Her voice rose barely above a murmur, almost drowned out by the night sounds.

He eased his hold on her and cradled her face in his hands. The most unbearable longing shone in his eyes. Any moment now he would kiss her, and she hungered for that kiss with every cell of her body. Urgency choked her until she couldn't swallow, couldn't even breathe. In those few seconds, she watched raw and powerful emotions flash across Kip's face—emotions that matched her own in intensity, emotions that made her want to claw away once and for all the protective mask he hid behind.

Because she could see he was about to don that mask again.

With a shudder, she pulled away and locked her arms across her chest. "What are you so afraid of, Kip Lorimer? I've told you my fears. Why won't you tell me yours?"

A ragged sigh shook him. "Because, unlike your Ernie Finston, who you've said is locked up in jail somewhere, the person who scares me most has this way of showing up when I least expect it. I'm afraid if I let down my guard and try to settle somewhere, she'll ruin it for me all over again."

She? A coldness crept into Sheridan's heart. A woman had hurt him this badly? No wonder he resisted the attraction they both knew grew stronger every moment they spent together. "That's why you left Texas?"

"That's why I left Texas. Why I'm never going back." The rising moon shimmered in his eyes as he cast a tentative glance toward Sheridan. "Classes start early in the morning. Better call it a night."

Unanswered questions tore at her as she watched him disappear around the side of the house. *Dear Jesus, I'm falling in love with that man. Help us both to overcome the fears that haunt us. Help us learn to trust again.*

And please, please let him stay!

During classes the next morning, Kip remained as polite as ever—and as closed-mouthed.

Yet every time they neared each other, Sheridan sensed his tension. It was all she could do to keep from dragging him behind the round pen and forcing him to explain why he couldn't admit he had feelings for her.

And she knew he did. She knew it down to her cramped toes aching to be free of thick socks and paddock boots.

On her way back from returning horses to the pasture with Manuelo, she glanced up to see Kip disappear into the caretaker's cottage, probably to grab some lunch before setting to work again. He'd straight out admitted how much he liked it here, but how much longer would he stay? Whoever *she* was—the woman he'd alluded to last night— she obviously caused him more than a little concern.

Something green and slimy churned in Sheridan's stomach. *Jealousy?* Of a woman she didn't even know? A woman who was clearly out of Kip's life—or so he seemed to hope.

"Manuelo," she said, following the stable hand into the barn, "do you and Kip talk much?"

"*No mucho, señorita.*" Manuelo uncoiled the hose to refill the water pails in the stalls.

"I thought he might have told you a little about his life back in Texas, his family and all." She peeked in on Sundown, a mahogany bay gelding on stall rest because of a sore hoof, and rubbed him between the eyes.

"*Señor* Kip does not say much." Manuelo shrugged and moved to the next stall with the hose.

"So . . . he's never mentioned an old girlfriend? An ex-wife, maybe?"

"No, *señorita.*" Manuelo paused and cast her a knowing grin. "You like *Señor* Kip, I think. I think *Señor* Kip likes you, too."

But enough to let go of his past and stick around? She feared the answer was no, and it made her angry all over again for allowing herself to trust someone who'd surely hurt her if she gave him the chance. Not in the same way as the Finstons, but maybe a whole lot worse.

Kip decided to skip church Sunday morning. It would be way too hard being that close to Sheridan. It had taken every ounce of willpower Friday night to walk away from her without devouring those lips that invaded his dreams by night and drove him to distraction by day. He'd stick around through the summer classes, like he'd promised, and then he'd leave.

He had to. He couldn't risk the heartbreak.

He leaned over the bathroom sink, his stomach cramping as memories steamrolled through his brain. The snap of a suitcase latch. The slamming of the trailer door. The muffled sobs through paper-thin walls when his daddy didn't know he could hear.

The past doesn't have to repeat itself.

His head jerked up. He peered at his cloudy reflection in the mirror, still fogged from his morning shower.

The past doesn't have to repeat itself.

Tears flooded his eyes. "Please, God, I want to believe it. Help me."

Kip prayed a lot over the next week and even asked Manuelo if he could borrow a Bible. On Wednesday afternoon, Manuelo brought Kip a dog-eared New Testament with Psalms. Accepting it with thanks, Kip invited the man in for a soft drink, and they sat together at Kip's small dinette.

Manuelo sipped from the frosty can. "You seek direction, *Señor* Kip?"

"Something like that." Kip ran his thumb along the edge of the Bible. The book fell open to Psalm 62, where someone had highlighted a verse: *Trust in him at all times, you people; pour out your hearts to him, for God is our refuge.*

Manuelo leaned across the table to see the page. A big grin lit his brown, furrowed face. "Already the Lord speaks to you."

Kip stretched out one blue-jeaned leg. "The other day you said the Lord had brought me and Gem here for a reason."

"*Sí*. To heal." Manuelo nudged his can aside and folded his arms on the table. "I think you hide from something, someone. Is why you come all this long way here from Texas."

Kip gave Manuelo a bemused half-smile. "That obvious, huh?"

Manuelo laughed softly. "I do not raise seven children and not learn to read signs."

The old gut-stabbing pain made Kip sit forward. "Maybe if my dad was still around, I wouldn't have so many questions."

Manuelo gave his head a sad shake. "He is not living?"

"Died when I was sixteen."

"And your mother?"

Kip drained his cola and stood. Crushing the can in one fist, he tossed it into the trashcan. Venom laced his next words. "I pray I never see that woman again as long as I live."

A sideways glance caught Manuelo's lowered head. "You should not speak so about the woman who gave you life."

"She *ruined* my life." And not just once. Over and over and over again, she'd managed to stir up trouble and draw Kip into it. He braced his hands on the back of his chair. "Believe me, I've got my reasons for hating my mother."

"Hate is no good, *Señor* Kip. You must pray to forgive." Manuelo rose and pressed a firm hand against Kip's forearm. "I pray for you, too." With a brisk nod, he dropped his empty cola can into the trash. "*Muchas gracias.* I will finish in the barn now."

Alone in the quiet cottage, Kip dug the heels of his hands into his eye sockets. How could God—how could *anyone*—hold it against him for hating his mother? Her desertion was what ultimately killed Kip's dad—and scarred

Kip with distrust for every other woman who came into his life.

Until Sheridan.

If only he could trust she'd never break his heart.

"You should come, Sheridan. It'll be fun." Janet Tippens, one of the teachers in Sheridan's class, cast her a hopeful smile through the ladies' room mirror.

"I don't know . . ." Sheridan tore off a paper towel and dried her hands. Janet had just invited her to join several of the teachers for a celebratory dinner at an upscale Charlotte restaurant that, for one thing, was way outside Sheridan's budget. For another . . . "I was planning to head back to Kingsley as soon as class ends tomorrow."

"It won't be a late evening." Janet gave a friendly wink. "And Greg would love to get to know you better."

All the more reason *not* to join the group. "Greg's really not my type. I'd hate to encourage him."

Janet slipped her purse strap up her arm and held the door. "I know he can be a little pushy. But he teaches at my school and I can promise you he's a nice guy."

"I'm sure he is, but seriously, I'm not interested."

Back in her seat, Sheridan fidgeted with her spiral notebook and pretended to take notes. She'd learned much that she could use in her teaching next fall. And this was her life's calling after all . . . wasn't it? Then why was she so ready for the two weeks to be over so she could get back to the farm?

It wasn't as if she could expect Kip to have changed his mind and would finally let her into his heart. Whatever wounds he bore from that mysterious *she* in his past, Sheridan began to doubt he'd ever fully heal.

A folded piece of paper slid into view over her right shoulder. With one eye on the instructor—wow, at twenty-eight years old was she engaging in junior-high note-passing?—she pretended to scratch the back of her neck and palmed the note. Lowering it to her lap, she carefully unfolded it.

Sheridan,

If I promise to be on my best behavior, will you give me another chance? Join me for dinner with the group tomorrow. Please?

—Greg

She felt his eyes drilling into her skull, even from three seats behind her. Well. Since Kip Lorimer seemed determined to shut her out of his life, maybe it was time to take herself off the shelf and try dating someone who actually showed a little courage and initiative.

Flipping over the note, she penned a quick response.

Greg—

Sorry I've been so cool. Nothing personal —just had a lot on my mind this summer. I would love to go to dinner with you.

—Sheridan

She "accidentally" dropped her pen on the floor, and as she bent to pick it up, she passed the note to the person behind her, then sat forward with an innocent smile. Her stomach somersaulted. Her palm left a clammy handprint on her notebook page.

Yep, junior high all over again.

"Easy, easy . . ." Nathan winced as Kip helped him slide his head and arms into a clean T-shirt, then refasten the cervical collar. "Man, I'm getting sick of this thing."

Kip handed Nathan the remote for his bedroom TV. "How much longer you gotta wear it?"

"We'll see what my doc says on Monday." He scooted onto the bed and arranged pillows against the headboard.

Kip resisted the urge to offer a hand. He knew Nathan well enough to recognize his I'd-rather-do-it-myself moods. "You still in much pain?"

"Not as bad lately." Nathan flipped through several TV channels before tossing the remote on the nightstand. "Nothing but reruns. Want to play some Scrabble?"

Kip smirked. "You're lookin' at the world's worst speller."

"I'm not averse to a little creative spelling, myself." Nathan nodded toward the dresser where the game sat. "Come on, humor me. I'll even spot you fifty points."

Kip shrugged. What did he have to lose, other than his self-respect? Nothing waited for him back at the cottage except a small-screen TV with bad reception and a pantry bare as Mother Hubbard's cupboard. He supposed he could suffer through a Scrabble game or two.

They set up the game on a small table next to the front

window. Following Nathan's instructions, Kip drew seven tiles and lined them up on the little plastic stand. Great, a *Q*, three *E*s, a *W*, *F*, and *A*. Nathan played first, laying down a twenty-six-point word that Kip couldn't even pronounce. "Is that even in the dictionary?"

Nathan quirked a grin. "You challenging me?"

"Not on your life." Kip studied the board. He could use Nathan's *C*, add his *A* and *W*, and make CAW. A few points anyway. He played the word and replaced his tiles. His gaze drifted toward the window while he waited for Nathan to take his next turn. The evening had taken on the golden hues of sunset. Long shadows stretched toward the east. A light breeze stirred the trees.

"She said she might be late."

"Huh?" Kip swung his head around.

Nathan clicked four more tiles into position. His chin bobbed as he mentally calculated his score. "You can't fool me, man. You're stuck on my sister."

Kip scraped stiff fingers through his hair and stared hard at his tiles. Like that would help. "You have a girlfriend?"

"Me? No. No one serious anyway. I've got some girl *friends* on campus I like to hang out with." Nathan gave his back a cautious stretch. "You need some help making a word?"

"I think I got one." He laid his *F* and two *E*s in front of an *L*.

Nathan chuckled. "I *feel* like you are avoiding talking about my sister."

"I *feel* like that ain't none of your business." Kip glared and drew three more tiles.

"Just trying to help you out, man." He quickly spelled

out SAFE using Kip's *F*. "You and Sher'd make a great couple."

Kip slapped the *U* and *N* he'd just drawn in front of Nathan's SAFE. "Unsafe. That's how I feel about relationships. With Sheridan or any other woman."

Didn't matter that he'd prayed about it all week. Didn't matter that he kept hearing those same words over and over in his head—*The past doesn't have to repeat itself*—like the voice of God Himself trying to break through Kip's resistance. Falling in love was for nice guys who'd grown up in a loving home with a mom who didn't leave.

Nathan eased his back. "If my sister trusts you enough to let her guard down, that's huge. Give Sher a chance. She's worth it."

Kip pushed his chair away from the table. Images of Sheridan danced through his thoughts. The first time they met and the way she'd stubbornly insisted on his references. The night of the storm when she'd pulled the sliver from his foot. The feel of her soft curves as he held her to him just one week ago.

No forty-seven ways to Sunday about it, he was head-over-his-boot-heels in love, and he might as well admit it.

Chapter Eleven

Someone was telling a teacher joke, and Sheridan missed the punch line. She was too busy fending off Greg. If he scooted his chair any closer, he'd be sitting on her lap. Or have her on his. And that was totally *not* happening.

"Whew! Is it warm in here, or is it just me?" Sheridan fanned herself and reached for her water glass.

Greg's hot breath scalded her ear. "Maybe we should take a walk, get some air."

"Actually, I should be getting home. My dog has been cooped up since noon." After missing Xena so much last week, Sheridan had brought her along this time.

The server came around to return credit cards and change. Greg pocketed his card and receipt. "I'd love to meet your dog. What kind is it?"

"She's a Great Dane."

Greg laughed. "I pictured you as more the chihuahua type. I've got a feisty little Jack Russell, myself." He ran his hand up and down Sheridan's arm. His gaze softened. "So can I come over for a bit? We could walk your dog together and talk where it's less crowded."

She should say no. She *wanted* to say no. Greg was too presumptuous for his own good, but the puppy-dog look in his eyes began to work its charm. Besides, hadn't she already convinced herself it was pointless to hold out hope for Kip? Why waste time pining over the unattainable when a chance for a real relationship stared her in the face? And the guy liked dogs, after all. That was a good sign, wasn't it?

"All right, but I really do have to make it an early evening. My mom's expecting me back at the farm tonight."

Greg checked his watch. "It's just now seven thirty. How about if you're on the road by nine?"

"Fair enough."

As they entered Sheridan's townhouse twenty minutes later, a deep bark sounded from somewhere overhead. Xena barreled down the stairs, almost colliding with Greg in the entryway. The big dog skidded to a halt on the parquet flooring, the hair along her spine standing up like a Mohawk. A low growl vibrated in her throat.

"Nice doggy." Greg took a quick step backward. "Wow. She really is big. She could finish off my little fella in two bites."

"She's harmless, I promise." Sheridan stepped to the hall closet and grabbed Xena's leash and a couple of disposable doggy waste bags. "Ready for that walk?"

By now, Xena was dancing and prancing and yipping with excitement. Her wagging tail slapped against the wall, the newel post, the hall table . . .

"Hold still, will you?" Sheridan struggled to fasten Xena's leash—not easy with a moving target. She tried snapping her fingers and looking stern, but that only excited Xena more. "What's the deal? You always behave perfectly when Kip—"

Sheridan's stomach twisted. She dropped her hands to her sides and heaved a frustrated groan.

"Here, let me try." With minimal effort and probably the element of surprise as much as anything, Greg clipped the leash to Xena's collar. She immediately quieted and sat on her haunches. "See? Not so hard. You want me to walk her?"

"Why not?" Sheridan swallowed her sarcasm and held the door. "The park around the corner has a nice area for pets."

They strolled down the sidewalk with Xena prancing in front of them, the evening sun making her shadow look ten feet tall.

"Slow down, girl. This isn't a race." Greg gave the leash a quick tug. "So who's this Kip person? Your dog trainer?"

"He's my mom's new barn manager." Sheridan's toes hurt. She wished she'd changed into her padded flip-flops, but she really just wanted to get this "date" over with.

"Tell me more about the farm. You said you hold riding therapy classes?"

"We're fully accredited, with licensed instructor-therapists and a whole crew of dedicated volunteers." They'd reached the park, and Sheridan pointed to the left, where a grassy area had been fenced off for dogs.

Inside the enclosure, Sheridan released Xena to romp with her doggy friends. Sheridan and Greg followed at a leisurely walk, and she didn't resist when he took her hand.

"Thanks for giving me a chance." Greg flashed Sheridan a crooked grin.

She smiled slightly. "You're a hard man to say no to, Greg Mason."

"I like the sound of that." Greg led Sheridan over to a

bench and drew her next to him, pulling her under his arm. "I really want to keep seeing you. Would that be okay?"

Sheridan locked her fingers together to keep them from trembling. Cactus-like prickles set every nerve on edge. Greg's lips grazed her cheek, and she caught a whiff of the decaf he'd been sipping earlier—a stale, musty smell blending with the remnants of a breath mint.

"Sher?" He eased his other arm around her, enclosing her. His steamy breath whispered across her ear. "I mean it. Do you think—"

"Xena! No!" Shoving out of Greg's embrace, Sheridan launched herself off the bench and tore over to where Xena gnawed on something dead—a toad, by the looks of it. "Bad dog! Yucky!" She used one of the waste bags to dispose of the nearly petrified corpse, then stood staring into the trashcan while she fought to bring her breathing back to normal.

Sensing a presence behind her, she turned to see Greg standing there. "I came on way too strong, didn't I?" He peered shyly up at her. "I can't help myself when I'm around you, Sher. You're special. You're everything I've ever wanted in a woman."

"Oh, Greg, how can you say that? You hardly know me."

"I know enough to know I want to know more." He cradled her hand. "Please. Say you'll see me again."

"I don't know. Maybe." Freeing herself, Sheridan shook her head and snapped the leash onto Xena's collar. "It's almost dark. I need to get back."

On the tiny porch outside her front door, Sheridan stood motionless while Greg planted an awkward kiss on her cheek. Hands in his pockets, he stepped off the porch and turned, his face catching the amber glow of the porch light. "So . . . can I call you? When will you be back in town?"

"Probably not until school starts. I'll be helping with the therapy classes the rest of the summer." Sheridan unlocked the door and sent Xena inside.

"Maybe I could visit you at the farm."

"Maybe." *Please don't.*

"Well, good night."

"Good night. Thanks for dinner and . . . everything." Sheridan shot him a forced smile before hurrying inside and falling against the closed door.

Jowls dripping after a long drink from her water bowl, Xena strode over and planted her wet muzzle against Sheridan's belt. Those big, expressive doggy eyes bored holes through her.

"I know, I know. He's not Kip. But he's not so bad, huh? We could do worse."

Kip didn't know which was worse, fighting his feelings for a woman he couldn't have or watching that woman make goo-goo eyes at a citified wimp in Bermuda shorts.

Actually, it was the wimp making eyes at Sheridan. He'd shown up at the farm along about mid-morning Saturday, driving one of those close-to-the-ground sports cars with fancy chrome wheel rims and racing stripes down the sides. Kip first thought he must be the dad or uncle of one of their Saturday kids—until he'd asked Kip where to find Sheridan. And in a tone of voice that implied a certain . . . possessiveness.

And it rankled him. Big-time.

"Kip? Kip! How about some help here?"

At the sound of Mrs. Cross's annoyed tone, he snapped his head around. The stiff brush he'd been grooming Belle with hit the barn floor with a thud. "Sorry. Whatcha need, ma'am?"

She frowned at him in disbelief. Only then did he notice how she struggled beneath the weight of a Western saddle. He hurried over and relieved her of the burden.

Mrs. Cross followed him into the tack room. "You seem a wee bit preoccupied this morning. Nothing to do with our visitor, I'm sure."

"Visitor?" Bracing the saddle on one knee, Kip tugged the saddle blanket loose from underneath before plopping the saddle onto the rack. He shook out the blanket and turned it upside down over the saddle.

"Don't play dumb with me." Mrs. Cross examined a bridle. "I've been watching you watching Greg all morning."

Greg, huh? Kip snatched a kerchief from his back pocket and mopped his neck. "I should finish up with Belle. You'll need her in the next class."

"Kip." The woman's tone was plenty by itself to stop him in his tracks, but her firm grip on his forearm ensured she meant business. "I know you have feelings for my daughter. I know she has feelings for you. And I know something happened between you last weekend that sent her back to the city intent on putting you out of her life. If there's something I should know about—something that affects our working relationship or especially if it threatens my family in any way—"

"I'd never intentionally hurt your daughter or anyone else. And I love working here more than I ever thought possible." Kip tugged off his Stetson and kneaded the brim, his fingers pressing deep into the woven straw. "It's true, I do have feelings for Sheridan. But I'm scared of rushing into anything. I need to make sure—"

How could he explain the fear that someday when he least expected it, the past would come crashing into the present, destroying his life all over again?

"Mom, you in here?" Sheridan peered into the tack room. "Cindy's ready for Belle—" Her gaze found Kip's. "Am I interrupting something?"

"Just getting Belle's tack." Mrs. Cross sent Kip a pointed stare, a clear sign they'd take up this conversation again later.

Chores finished, the fridge restocked, boots off, and the latest issue of *Horse & Rider* in hand, Kip plopped into the easy chair. From here he had a clear view of the driveway behind the main house. And there sat that infernal little sports car.

A motion caught his eye—Sheridan stepping out the back door, with Greg the Life-sized Ken Doll right behind her. The creep pulled her close and whispered something in her ear. She immediately threw off his hand and marched across the porch.

Two seconds later, Greg cornered her at the rail, his hands sliding up her arms, cradling her face, moving in for a kiss. Kip's insides boiled. His breath sliced in and out like a rusty knife blade. He tossed aside the magazine. *Don't do it, Sher. Don't—*

Suddenly she drew both arms up and shoved the guy hard in the chest. He stumbled backward, looking confused.

Well, Kip wasn't the least bit confused. He tore out the

door and sprinted across the yard. He bounded up the porch steps and clutched the creep by the lapels of his carnation-pink polo shirt. "Looks to me like the lady said no, Mister Roamin' Hands. What part of that don't you understand?"

"Cool it, okay?" Greg grabbed Kip's wrists. His twisted grin spoke a sick combination of fear and false bravado.

Kip's knuckles tingled with the urge to punch that grin right off the guy's face. "You're the one who needs to cool it."

"Kip, it's okay."

Sheridan's soft touch on his arm forced him to swallow and suck in a steadying breath. He dropped his hands to his sides and wiggled his fingers.

He felt like a fool.

"I, uh . . . Sorry, this was none of my business. I just—"

"You're right about that!" So Greg was back to Mr. Tough Guy. He straightened his shirt. "You've got some nerve, cowboy. You should—"

"Stop it, Greg." Arms crossed, Sheridan stepped between him and Kip. "I think you should go now."

"But we were just getting better acquainted." Greg's tone turned all mushy, just like his saccharine-sweet smile. Kip imagined shoving him head first into a manure pile.

Sheridan cast a quick pleading glance over her shoulder at Kip. He took the hint and edged away, but not so far that he couldn't catch Sheridan's next words to the pathetic excuse for a boyfriend.

"I'm sorry, Greg," she murmured. "You asked me to give you a chance and I did. But I'm not ready for the kind of relationship you want. Please leave. And don't call me again." She turned her back on him and gazed into the gathering dusk.

Greg shot Kip a blistering glare on his way down the porch steps. He folded himself into the seat of his toy car and spewed gravel as he sped toward the gate.

Kip propped a hip against the porch rail. Disgust filled him—for Greg's audacity and for his own out-of-control temper. "Guess I ruined your evening."

Sheridan curled her lips into a sad smile. "You aren't the one who ruined my evening. I managed to do that all by myself."

Kip scooted closer and braced both hands on the porch rail. "So . . . who exactly was that guy?"

"Just a teacher I met at my class." Her fingers crept along the rail, stopping inches from his. "He likes dogs."

"That so?" Kip spread his hand until his little finger grazed hers.

"Proves I can't trust my own judgment, I guess. Or my dog's."

"I don't know . . . Xena seems pretty smart to me."

"She likes you, that's for sure." Sheridan's soft laughter rippled. "Actually, she did raise her hackles and growl at Greg when they were first introduced."

"Knew I liked that dog." Kip stared at her hand. His voice got stuck somewhere behind his Adam's apple. "Sher, about last weekend . . ."

She swiveled to face him. Her eyes grew dreamy and soft, and it seemed he could see clear down to her soul. A knowing smile parted her lips. Luscious lips, pink like strawberries and cream. "You ready to tell me why you suddenly turned tail and ran instead of kissing me like I knew you wanted to?" she asked.

He still wanted to. He wanted to find out if those lips tasted as sweet as they looked. Like an irresistible force, they enticed him closer, closer. His right hand slipped behind her waist, his left hand cradled the back of her head. His mouth hovered over hers, the anticipation swelling until it felt like his heart would burst right out of his chest.

Slowly, slowly he lowered his lips to hers. Their velvety softness sent shockwaves through him, stealing his breath, robbing him of reason. It took every last ounce of restraint to keep from crushing her against him and kissing her senseless.

Shaking, breathless, but oh so unwillingly, he broke away. He chuckled softly and shook his head. "What were we talking about?"

Chapter Twelve

Talking? They were *talking*? Sheridan's brain had left for La-la Land about the time Kip leaned in for that kiss. Her legs had morphed into overcooked spaghetti. "That was . . ."

"Yeah." Kip sounded as stunned as she felt. He tugged her over to the porch swing, where they sat hip to hip in breathless silence. Weaving his fingers through hers, he nudged the swing into motion.

Glimpsing his bare feet, she laughed. "That's twice now I've seen you storm the ramparts with your boots off."

Kip wiggled his toes, then angled her a one-eyed glare. "So you aren't *too* mad at me for rescuing you from that punk with the toy car?"

"Would you believe I planned the whole thing just so you'd kiss me like you just did?"

He lifted an eyebrow. "Did you?"

She answered with a noncommittal shrug. Maybe she did plan it, in a way. All day long she couldn't help wondering what must be going through Kip's mind, watching another man openly flirt with her. And did he happen to notice she never actually flirted back?

Greg's fawning attention grew more tiresome the longer she was around him, yet she'd allowed him to stay, maybe even encouraged him if she were completely honest. They'd watched a rented DVD, played Scrabble with Nathan, and taken a walk down the lane. She'd even let him hold her hand. And she hardly batted an eye when Mom suggested Greg join them for supper.

Hmm. Knowing Mom, she'd probably pegged the situation from the start.

Well, intentional or not, it worked. And now Sheridan couldn't keep the smug smile off her face. "I'm thirsty. How about you? Mom made some fresh-squeezed lemonade today. Nice and tart."

Kip grinned. "Kinda like you?"

She rose from the swing and pulled him up beside her. "Exactly. And don't you forget it."

The week sped by in a glorious blur. Sheridan couldn't remember when she'd been so happy to be back at the farm. In the aftermath of the Finstons, her parents had worked hard to convince Sheridan that not every stranger she met posed a threat. Even so, her teen years had been haunted by restless nights and terrifying dreams.

Going away to college brought her first relief from the nightmares. It helped having three suite-mates, a solid lock on the door, and a security guard on duty day and night. After landing her first teaching job, she'd leased a townhouse in a gated community and eventually adopted Xena, who at least *looked* scary. With the passage of time and a satisfying teaching job in hand, she felt she'd finally started living a semi-normal existence.

But since her father's death, Sheridan couldn't shake her worries about Mom living alone so far from help. And whenever Sheridan returned to the farm for weekends, holidays, or summer vacations, the disturbing memories returned.

Except she hadn't experienced a bad night all week. In fact, all her dreams seemed to focus on one very wonderful, completely adorable, utterly amazing cowboy.

She'd just slipped on the open-toed mules that matched her new sleeveless print dress when Mom peeked into her room. "Ready for church, honey? Kip's waiting in the kitchen."

A rush of warmth swept through her. "Be down in a sec."

Mom paused in the doorway. "Would you stop by Nathan's room? He's acting a bit glum this morning."

A knot of concern tightened beneath Sheridan's breastbone. The words *glum* and *Nathan* didn't go together at all. She gave herself a mental chewing-out. So wrapped up in her budding relationship with Kip, she'd remained shamefully unaware of much else going on around her.

She snatched her purse and linked her arm through her mother's. "I bet it's just the frustration of being out of commission for the summer. Nothing keeps Nathan down for long."

At the foot of the stairs, Sheridan turned down the hall toward Nathan's room. The door stood ajar, so she tapped lightly before stepping inside. "Hey, bro."

"Hey." Nathan sat propped up in bed flipping channels with the remote. He still wore the plaid boxers and T-shirt he'd slept in. His thick, wiry hair was scrunched up on one side, and a whiskery shadow darkened his jaw.

Sheridan crossed her arms and hoped her stern glare masked the genuine concern churning inside her. "Mom says you're not going to church. What gives, lazybones?"

"Not in the mood." He punched the OFF button and tossed the remote onto the nightstand. "Hand me my iPad, will you?"

Sheridan followed his pointing finger to where he'd left the device on the table by the window. She turned toward him with a raised eyebrow. "Get it yourself. Better yet, get your sorry rear out of that bed and get ready for church. And make it snappy. We're already running late."

"Mom sent you in here, didn't she? Tell her to quit worrying and just leave me alone."

Sheridan blew out a long, slow sigh. "You know perfectly well that *worry* is a four-letter word with Mom. So if she *is* worried, then she has good reason. And now I'm worried, too. So out with it. What's up with you this morning?"

Nathan groaned and clawed his temples. "Can't a guy have a lousy day once in a while?"

"Nathan Cross does not *have* lousy days. Nathan Cross is the king of good cheer." Sheridan stepped closer and forced him to give her his hand. She squeezed it hard. "So if Nathan Cross is grumpy, the world wants to know why."

"You wanna know why? Okay, I'll tell you." Nathan's tone grew harsh. "This is turning out to be one monster of a summer. I'm laid up with a broken wrist and a cracked neck bone. Can't ride, can't help with the therapy classes, can't do much of anything but sit here and vegetate." He snatched back his hand and stared out the window. "So get out of here. You'll be late for church."

Sheridan crossed her arms. "Quite a pity party you've got going on there."

"And you're not invited."

Stung to the core and confused by this seldom-seen side of her brother, she marched to the kitchen.

Mom and Kip looked up from the table, where they sat sipping coffee. "Would he talk to you?" Mom asked.

"Being out of commission for so long is really getting to him." Sheridan stood behind Kip's chair, her hands on his shoulders. The feel of his taut muscles beneath her fingers helped replenish her sapped strength. "But you know Nathan. I'm sure he'll be back to his old self before we get home from church."

They started out to the garage. Mom handed Kip the keys to her Tahoe and asked him to drive. Sheridan took the front passenger seat, and Mom climbed in behind her. They rode in thoughtful silence for a couple of miles, until Kip finally spoke. "Maybe I shouldn't say anything, but . . . I have an idea what's really bothering Nathan."

Sheridan studied Kip's profile. "You know something we don't?"

"Yes, tell us, Kip," Mom urged. "You almost spend more time with him than either of us do."

Kip slowed for a stop sign. After checking traffic, he continued on toward town. "I think Nathan's afraid."

Sheridan tucked in her chin. "Afraid of what? His doctor gave him a good report, said his neck and wrist were healing right on schedule."

"It's that old thing about getting back on the horse that threw you." Kip rubbed his jaw. "Nathan's been hinting around about giving up riding. One day he even asked what I thought a horse like Jet would sell for."

Mom gasped. "Nathan would never part with his father's horse. All he's ever wanted was to ride like his dad."

"I'm just tellin' you my suspicions."

Sheridan stared unseeing at the passing landscape as she pieced together a collage of memories from the past few weeks. Watching Kip work Jet in the round pen. Marveling at the daily progress Jet made as Kip put him through his paces in the jump arena.

And—now that she really thought about it—the daily changes in Nathan as he gradually went from enthusiasm about having a professional horseman take over Jet's training to the realization that the horse was doing things for Kip that Nathan couldn't even dream of.

Several more minutes of silence passed, until Mom gave an annoyed sniff. "If you knew this was bothering Nathan so badly, I wish you'd have told me."

"Didn't see it as my place. Figured if Nathan wanted to talk to y'all about it, he would."

"Mom, Kip is right. Nathan isn't a kid anymore. We have to respect his privacy." Sheridan reached around the seat to pat her mother's leg.

Mom sighed. "It's just so hard watching your children go through trials and knowing there's nothing you can do to fix things for them."

Sheridan felt the love in her mother's words, the pain and the regret. She remembered a few weeks ago when Mom shared how a parent's love mirrored the love of God for His children—and how trusting in God's perfect love gave her the faith to face each day.

She swiveled to smile over her shoulder. "How about we have a little faith, Mom? Like you've told me time and again, after all God's done for us already, I believe we can trust Him to heal Nathan inside and out."

Mom's lips creased into a sad smile. "Well, well, look who's found her faith wings."

"About time, huh?" Before facing forward, Sheridan cast a quick glance at Kip, and her heart skittered. What if God hadn't brought him to their farm this summer? How different might her life be right this minute?

A flash of Greg Mason's roving hands and hot breath made her shiver with revulsion. No, she'd stay single forever if that was the best she could do.

Temptation on two legs—that about described Sheridan Cross. Blond, blue-eyed, and more beautiful than the sky at sunrise on a crystal summer morning. Kip stole glances at her all through the church service, hardly able to believe how God had blessed him! Only the Creator of the universe could have orchestrated the series of events that had brought Kip all the way from Nacogdoches, Texas, to Kingsley, North Carolina, on a whim. The Lord indeed worked in mysterious ways.

And none so mysterious as the love of a man for a woman. Kip had promised himself way back when he first hit puberty that he'd never, ever trust his heart to a woman's wiles. Yet here he sat, lovesick as a moonfaced calf. He barely heard the pastor's sermon while one phrase played through his brain like a stuck recording: *Praise the Lord, I think she loves me!*

He did manage to divert his thoughts long enough during prayer time to lift up Nathan. He'd have been blind not to notice the subtle shift in Nathan's attitude over the past couple of weeks. While he hadn't come right out and told Nathan he was way out of his depth with a horse like

Jet, he'd seen Nathan watching them at work. To anybody with an ounce of horse sense, the differences in their skill levels would be as plain as the white four-pointed star on Jet's face.

What concerned Kip most was that Nathan might be too intimidated to ever ride again. Somehow, some way, Kip had to get the boy back on a horse as soon as his doctor allowed. One of the therapy horses would be best, but Kip had a feeling such a suggestion would only insult Nathan's pride.

Nope, he had to find exactly the right mount for Nathan—a horse that matched his fun-loving spirit while providing just enough challenge for his riding abilities. Too bad Kip hadn't had time to make more connections in the area. Back in Nacogdoches his training and saddle-making business had netted him all kinds of horse-related contacts.

Thoughts of Nacogdoches reminded him of Tom Jacobs. If anybody knew horses, it was Tom, and Kip suspected he could describe Nathan's abilities over the phone and Tom could walk out to his herd and pick the perfect horse. Yep, he'd have to give Tom a call later.

If his brain didn't turn to mush from kissing Sheridan Cross. How long before he could get her alone again and hold her in his arms like he'd done last night? Oh, mercy, if the preacher knew Kip was thinking about kissing the girl of his dreams instead of dwelling on the Word of God, he'd be thrown out of church on his ear.

And then, like the whisper of a breeze, a new thought filled his mind: *I invented love.*

Kip lowered his head and let God's peace roll over him. *Yes, Lord, You certainly did. Grant me the courage to believe it's possible for me.*

It seemed wise to keep his idea to himself for now, so Kip waited until Monday evening, when he was alone in the cottage, to ring up Tom Jacobs.

"Well, glory be! How are you, son? Tried to phone your cell a couple of times but guess you changed your number. You get to North Carolina okay?"

Tom's lusty greeting brought a smile to Kip's face. He settled deeper into the easy chair and propped one bare foot on the ottoman. "It's beautiful country out here. Nice folks, too."

"Good, good, glad to hear it. That equine therapy center work out for Gem?"

"He loves it, made himself right at home." Kip sighed in lingering amazement over the changes in his life. "Same for me. The lady who runs the center hired me as her barn manager."

"Oh, yeah, the lady who called for references?"

"Actually, that was the daughter." Even Kip could tell how his voice got all soft and mellow and smiley at the mention of Sheridan.

Tom gave a low chuckle. "She sounded mighty pretty."

"That she is." *And I'm sitting here grinning and red-faced like a lovesick schoolboy.*

"Sounds like North Carolina is treating you all right—in more ways than one."

After a few more minutes of catching up, Kip explained about Nathan. "I don't have the connections here like I had in Texas, so I hoped you could help me out."

"Hmm, got a couple of my boys in mind that might be just the ticket. You remember that spunky bay I picked up at auction last year, the Morgan/quarter horse mix?"

"Ember? Smart as a whip, a real athlete, and a playful side, too." Kip gazed at the ceiling, seeing the gelding in his mind's eye, remembering the feel of the horse beneath his saddle. "Yep, he'd be a good one for Nathan."

"If you think so, I'll give your friend a good price and we can figure out how to get Ember out there."

That would be the hard part—if he didn't count the convincing it would take to get Nathan excited about trying out a new mount. Kip scratched his chin. "Nathan won't be up to riding again until summer's end at the earliest, so we've got time to work out the details. Maybe find someone heading this way who'd have room in his trailer."

"I'll keep my ears open." Tom grew silent for a moment. "By the way, when I was in the ranch supply store the other day, I ran into someone who's looking for you. She was mighty sorry to learn you'd left town."

Kip's stomach hit bottom. "She give her name?"

"Didn't think to ask. She had a girl with her, though— I'm assuming her daughter. She had one of your business cards so I figured she was looking to get a saddle made."

Kip's stomach completed its loop-de-loop and leveled off. He hauled in a relieved breath and blew it out again.

"I gave her the names of a couple other custom saddle makers around here, but she didn't seem interested. Kept asking if I knew where to find you."

That uneasy feeling plowed through his gut once more. "Did you tell her?"

"I don't give out information like that without asking permission first. Now, if I see her again . . ."

"No." Kip planted both feet on the floor and sat forward. "I'm making a fresh start here, and I'd just as soon keep the past in the past."

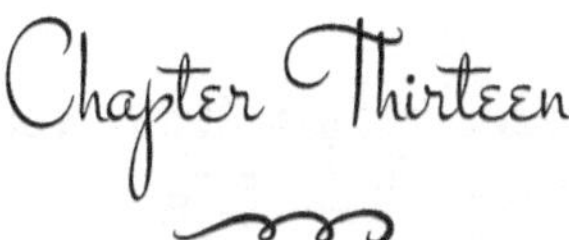

Chapter Thirteen

Sheridan couldn't get over how quickly Kip had taken to that tough kid Ryan. On Tuesday morning she'd watched them head out to the pasture together to fetch Gem, trading good-natured jabs and hearty laughter the whole way—over what, Sheridan wasn't sure she wanted to know. Guy stuff, probably.

But she loved seeing Kip laugh, and loved how he'd begun to relax and open up. He really started to seem at home at the farm. Oh, how she hoped he'd stay!

"Sher." Mom's voice startled her. "Are you planning on staring out at the pasture all morning or helping your rider?" She flicked a hand toward the center of the arena. "Pam's waiting to groom Lady."

"Sorry, Mom. I . . . got distracted."

Mom gave her a knowing smile. "So I noticed."

The quiet preteen Sheridan had been working with this summer stood a few feet in front of Lady with crossed arms and a furrowed brow. As Sheridan neared, the volunteer holding the horse's lead rope cast her a helpless glance. "Pam's being difficult today," she whispered.

Drawing in a fortifying breath, Sheridan laid her hands on the girl's shoulders. "What's wrong, not in the mood to groom your horse?"

Pam stared at the toes of her sneakers and shook her head hard.

"That's too bad, because Lady told me she's been waiting all week to see you again."

The girl sent Sheridan a withering look. "That's silly."

"Oh, so Lady hasn't talked to you before? She talks to me all the time." At Pam's raised eyebrow, Sheridan went on, "Not with human words, naturally, but in horse language."

"Horse language?" A flicker of curiosity brightened Pam's eyes.

"Come on, I'll show you." Sheridan draped an arm around Pam and nudged her closer to Lady. The horse nickered and pressed her muzzle into Sheridan's outstretched hand for a brisk nose rub. She smirked at Pam. "Do I need to translate that for you?"

Pam gave an exaggerated shrug. "I guess it means, 'Hello. I like you. Would you scratch my nose?'"

"Very good! Now why don't you grab a curry and see what she says to you?" With a wink at the other volunteer, Sheridan guided Pam's hand in circular motions along the horse's neck. Lady leaned into the pressure with an appreciative groan.

"Hey! She does like me!" Pam gave Lady a smoochy kiss on the cheek.

"What did I tell you?" Sheridan glanced over her shoulder to see Kip helping Ryan groom Gem. Amazement filled her once again at the special bond between those three —a man, a boy, and a horse. Returning her attention to

Pam, she recalled how much this farm had meant to her dad.

Unexpected sadness swept through her. Her summer break was half over, and soon she'd return to her teaching job. Suddenly Charlotte seemed a million miles away, another life, another lifetime. How could she leave all this behind?

How could she ever leave Kip?

And now she was being just plain ridiculous. Charlotte wasn't that far. She could see Kip every weekend if she wanted to.

If she wanted to?

She wanted to see him 24/7/365!

You could give up teaching and help Mom full-time running Cross Roads Farm . . .

"Miss Sheridan?" Pam held up a grooming brush. "Is this the one I use next?"

"Oh. Right." Sheridan shook off her crazy thoughts. "Flick your wrist with each stroke to brush off the dirt and hair you just curried up, like this," she said, demonstrating.

They finished Lady's left side and moved around to her right. From here, Sheridan could peek straight across Lady's withers and keep an eye on Kip. Oh, the way that man moved! Lean and lithe and oh-so-good-looking.

"He's cute, huh?" Pam paused in her currying.

Sheridan snapped her head around, only to discover Pam gazing straight at Ryan. She laughed and ruffled the girl's hair. "Ryan is too old for you, young lady."

Pam huffed a longing sigh. "He's still cute." She shot Sheridan a toothy grin. "And I can tell who you're sweet on!"

Heat that had nothing to do with the summer day shot flames up Sheridan's neck. She exchanged looks with the volunteer holding the lead rope—and got no sympathy. "It's time to clean Lady's hooves."

Ryan tossed the stiff brush into the grooming bucket. "Do I pick Gem's hooves now?"

"What? Yeah, hooves." Kip adjusted his Stetson while tearing his gaze away from the pretty lady a few steps away. "Remember how to lift his foot?"

Ryan ran his hand down Gem's left foreleg, then gently pinched the tendon above the hoof. The horse obediently raised his leg. Ryan balanced the hoof on his thigh and set to work.

"Good job." Kip nodded his approval.

Observing the connection between boy and horse set Kip to thinking about his own childhood. Man, he missed his dad! Andy Lorimer knew how to treat horses, and he knew how to treat people.

Maybe that was the problem. Dad had been *too* patient with Mom, always giving her the benefit of the doubt, forgiving her every time she broke his heart . . . even knowing she'd eventually break it again.

And yet here Kip stood, on the verge of giving his own heart to a woman. He had to believe things could be different, that all women weren't like his mother. *Lord, I'm falling hard for Sheridan. Please don't let this be the biggest mistake of my life.*

When Ryan finished grooming Gem, Kip had him lead the horse around the arena, where other volunteers had laid out a trail course with ground poles, raised poles, and orange traffic cones. The object was to encourage cooperation and trust between human and horse. Kip recalled Ryan's first day, how both he and his horse had stumbled through a much simpler course—all because Ryan was too busy whining about why he didn't want to be there. What a difference a month made!

Walking with Ryan and Gem out to the pasture after class, Kip realized he'd miss the boy once the summer session ended. It would have been nice to have a little brother, someone to look out for, someone who'd look up to him.

Ryan led Gem a few feet into the pasture before unfastening the halter. As Gem ambled off to munch on grass, Ryan strode over to Kip. "What's the matter? I do something wrong?"

"No, you were fine."

"Then why are you frowning like you just bit into a rotten apple?"

Kip started for the gate, pausing to sock Ryan playfully on the arm. "Just thinkin' what a mess of a little brother you'd make."

Ryan punched him back, a snarky grin curling his lips. Then he heaved a noisy sigh. "Wish you *were* my big brother." Lowering his voice, he added, "Wish you were my dad."

"You have problems with your dad?" Kip held the gate open for Ryan, then shut it behind them.

"Problems? Right. Most of the time he's just passed out dead drunk."

"That how you ended up in the group home?"

"That, and my mom getting fed up with trying to keep me out of trouble." Ryan grimaced and ran the back of his hand under his nose. "I did some super-bad stuff. It's no wonder she didn't want me around anymore."

"I know what that's like." Kip picked up his pace, as if he could outrun the memories.

Ryan hustled to keep up. "You were a bad kid?"

Kip huffed a wry laugh. "Guess I was, at times." Yep, he'd done his share of acting out after his mother left. Even worse after Dad died. If not for the friends on the rodeo circuit who'd taken him under their wing, he might have ended up just like Ryan.

"Hey, you two." Sheridan strode toward them on long blue-jeaned legs that curved in all the right places. Her grin stretched across her lightly tanned face. "Good job with Gem today, Ryan."

"Thanks, Miss Sheridan." Was the boy actually blushing beneath that mop of dark hair? And being polite, too. Yes, indeed, Kip would take Ryan as his little brother in a heartbeat.

"Better head to the bus. They're loading up." Sheridan fell into step with Kip as Ryan jogged toward his group. She slid her hand into his. "You've done wonders with him."

Kip drew her to a halt and faced her, taking both her hands. He tried to swallow, but his throat wouldn't work. "Maybe . . . maybe we should talk later."

"About what?" Her gaze searched his, and he felt like he could dive headfirst into those blue, blue eyes.

He hitched a breath. "It feels like we're heading toward something pretty special. I want all my cards on the table so you can decide once and for all if you really want to get mixed up with a guy like me."

"That sounds serious." She moved closer and rested her hands against his chest. "Anyway, I thought we already had something pretty special."

"Believe me, we do!" Kip's words rasped out with a

shudder. He couldn't take his eyes off her lips, parted just slightly, so full and pink and inviting . . .

Breeeeeeep! The school bus horn nearly knocked Kip out of his boots. Gasping, he waved at the driver, then led Sheridan toward the barn, where volunteers were busy putting away equipment and grooming kits.

A middle-aged woman struggled with a stack of traffic cones. Guess the kiss—and their much-needed talk—would have to wait. Kip heaved a sigh. "Duty calls."

By the time they stowed the gear and saw to the horses, Sheridan had gone to the house. Kip showered and changed, fixed himself a sandwich, and sat down at the table with the list of supplies he'd been adding to. Fly spray, a replacement feed bucket for the one Sundown tore up, a new gate latch for pasture two, a bag of grain . . .

His thoughts drifted to Sheridan again. God was working hard to convince him that whole "sins of the mother" thing didn't have to play out in Kip's future. Sandwiching time together between classes and chores, he and Sheridan had spent the last several days getting to know each other better. Now Kip needed to find the courage to tell her everything about his past.

He finished his lunch, jotted a few items on a grocery list, slapped on his Stetson, and strode out to his pickup. Best take care of business while he still had a few brain cells intact. Because if he waited around to see Sheridan first, he might not be able to stop kissing her until they both had to come up for air.

First stop, the farm supply store. Kip parked out front and bounded up the steps to the broad covered porch. The woodsy-grassy-leathery smells pricked his senses and, as always, brought an extra spring to his step. Nothing he liked better than the scent of fresh hay and grain.

Well, maybe *one* thing . . .

This was no time to get distracted. Time enough for kissing later.

On the way into the store, he detoured over to the community bulletin board. He'd been itching to get his custom saddle business going again and wanted to check out the competition.

A sullen girl blocked the narrow aisle. Hair the color of straw hung in a messy braid down her back. Arms locked across her ribcage, she stared at a display of horse supplements. Seemed a good guess she wasn't reading labels. In fact, she looked as though a feed store was the last place on earth she wanted to be.

Kip debated whether to excuse himself and edge past her or back up and take the next aisle. He was about to choose the latter when the girl hauled in a breath and snarled, "Mom! Can we go now? *Please?*"

"Patience, honey, patience."

Kip recognized the voice seconds before the woman it belonged to rounded the corner.

"If he's anywhere around here, this is—" The woman froze, her gaze ramming into Kip's. Joy, fear, hope, and shame collided and coalesced and coursed out in a moan. "Kip . . . my Kip!"

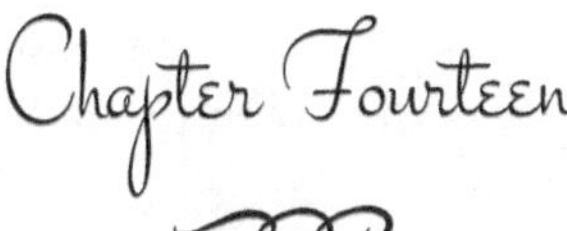

Chapter Fourteen

Sheridan caught Manuelo just before he started up the tractor to drag the arena. "Do you know where Kip went?"

"To buy supplies, I think. You need something, *señorita*?"

"Just wondering when he'll be back." She pursed her lips. He'd looked so serious this morning when he said they needed to talk.

"When I see him, I will tell him you look for him."

She waved her thanks and then herded Xena and Beau out of the arena as the tractor engine grumbled and kicked on. Leaving the two dogs to their play, she wandered over to the caretaker's cottage. She hadn't been inside since Kip moved in. She paused near the door and hugged herself against a shiver. All over again, she felt the tug of duct tape binding her wrists and ankles, the suffocating terror when Ernie slapped a strip across her mouth.

She turned away, bile rising into her throat along with the vile taste of Dell's peanut butter cookies.

Someday . . . someday she'd get over the memories. Someday she'd feel safe again.

And she did feel safe every time Kip held her in his arms. Thinking of him brought a gentle sigh to her lips. She stared down the lane, hoping for a glimpse of his battered white pickup.

Then an idea came to her. They hadn't had a real date yet. And since Kip was already in town, Sheridan could join him and they could grab a bite to eat and maybe have that little talk at Kingsley City Park, away from the prying eyes and ears of her mother and brother.

She jogged back to the house and hurried upstairs, where she changed into a pair of capris and a pastel cotton top, then ran a comb through her hair and dabbed on a little makeup. And a spritz of her favorite scent for good measure.

Common sense suggested she should call Kip before she left and make sure he wasn't already on his way home. After four rings, she expected the call to go to voicemail when Kip suddenly came on the line.

"Yeah?"

"Kip?" Sheridan's stomach clenched at the brusque sound of his voice. "Are—are you okay?"

He stammered something unintelligible—a curse? "I need to call you back."

He was definitely *not* okay. "Kip, what's wrong?"

Tense, heavy breathing filled her ear. A car door slammed. Men's voices. Laughter. Tires on gravel. A siren in the distance.

Sheridan clutched her phone with both hands. "Kip?"

"I can't talk right now. I promise I'll explain later."

"No! I can tell you're upset. Where are you? I'm on my way." Even as she spoke, she grabbed her purse and started downstairs.

He heaved another pained breath before murmuring,

"Okay, okay. Meet me at Kingsley Station. We're—I'm headed there now."

The line went dead.

We? He'd distinctly started to say, "*We're* headed there now."

Suddenly the serious talk Kip had hinted at earlier took on new significance. She couldn't get to Kingsley fast enough.

Kip stood next to the green Dodge rattletrap parked two slots over from his pickup. A cold lead weight sank deep into the pit of his stomach as he shoved his cell phone into his jeans pocket. His mother looked up at him with apology in her eyes, along with a plea for understanding. The girl—his *sister?*—leaned against the fender with a sneer on her face.

How could he not have known he had a little sister?

She looked about fifteen, and she'd definitely inherited their father's straw-blond hair and stubborn chin. So his mother must have been pregnant when she left. Just took off for parts unknown and never looked back, never cared what torment she'd abandoned her husband and son to endure in her wake.

He could barely stand to look at his mother. He let his gaze drift toward the girl. Grace Lorimer—except his mother said their name was Lawton now. The soft-looking girl with round cheeks appeared just a tad overweight. Her jeans showed a glimpse of a pudgy kneecap through shredded fabric. A faded red T-shirt bore some rock band logo, no longer readable. She wore scuffed brown roper boots and a cheap-looking tooled leather belt with a gaudy brass buckle.

Though his mother had started hanging with a different crowd after leaving Dad, she'd never strayed far from the rodeo circuit. Still skinny as a fence post but showing her age, she wore a green polo shirt over stretchy-looking jeans and gray snakeskin boots. The white-blond hair brushing her shoulders looked fried, with dark roots peeking through around her scalp. She reeked of cigarette smoke.

Kip ground his teeth. Might as well get this over with. "Kingsley Station is right downtown. You can follow me over."

His mother reached for his arm with a trembling sigh. "I'm—I'm sorry, Kip. I mean it."

"Right." His jaw ached. His fist tightened around his pickup keys. He whipped a glance at Grace, not daring to say what he really felt.

His mother fished through the depths of a big beige purse until she found her car keys. "Get in, Gracie. Let's go."

The girl gave an exaggerated eye roll and pushed off the fender. She glared at Kip for a wrenching moment before turning her spiteful look on her mother. "Why? So you can dump me off on some dude I don't even know?"

So *that* was his mother's plan? Leave Grace with Kip? "Now wait a minute—"

"Get in that car right this minute, Grace Ann Lawton." His mother pointed a bony finger toward the passenger side and waited until the girl sullenly obeyed. Then she turned back to Kip and seized his wrist. "Please, son, help me out this one last time. For your sister's sake if not for me."

"Fine." He shook off her hand and marched to his pickup. Forget the supplies. Forget everything. He could probably even forget about staying on at Cross Roads Farm. Slicing pain arced through his chest. No way would he inflict his family problems on the Crosses. Even if it meant leaving North Carolina and giving up Sheridan forever.

Sheridan. Oh Lord, please help! How would he ever explain his mother's arrival—much less a sister he never knew he had?

Vaguely he recalled run-ins with his mother when she'd had a shy little girl clinging to her leg. Watching a friend's kid was the lie she'd used. Now she had some serious explaining to do.

He checked his rearview mirror, his stomach curdling as he caught sight of the green Dodge following him. Turning onto Main Street, he considered flooring the accelerator, losing his mother in traffic, and tearing out of Kingsley as fast as this old pickup would go.

But you have a sister!

He pounded a fist against the steering wheel. Something about the rebellious look in Grace's eyes awakened an urgency to protect her somehow—from their mother, from herself, from whatever had brought them all the way from Texas to find Kip.

He flicked on his turn signal and wheeled the pickup into a parking space in the lot next to Kingsley Station. The restaurant wasn't too busy on a Tuesday afternoon, thank goodness. Kip had no desire to parade his family troubles in front of the whole town.

At the hostess counter he asked for a table in the back. "Somewhere quiet?"

"Sure. Right this way." The teenage girl's perky attitude grated on Kip's chafed nerves.

When the hostess seated them in a corner booth, he

said, "I'm expecting a friend to join us shortly. Will you send her on back?"

"You bet." The hostess passed menus around and said their server would be with them in a moment.

Not that Kip had any appetite. In fact, he felt downright nauseated. He slid into the booth across from his mother and Grace and laid his Stetson on the window ledge.

"Who's this friend you're waiting on?" Kip's mother glanced around nervously. "I'd hoped we could talk in private."

"She's my . . . she's the daughter of my employer." Kip snatched a sugar packet and tapped it against his palm. "Seein' as how my situation is about to change drastically, I owe her an explanation about why I won't be staying on."

"You mean you're not settled?" His mother pushed a strand of bleach-blond hair behind her ear with fingers stained from chain smoking. She looked about ready to kill for another nicotine hit. "But I thought—"

A ponytailed girl in bib overalls came over with a tray of water glasses. "Y'all ready to order?"

"Nothing for me." Kip slid his unopened menu to the edge of the table.

His mother asked for a cup of coffee for herself and a cola for Grace.

As the server left, Kip glanced at Grace, who'd sunk deeper into the seat, her arms folded in defiance. He shifted sideways and glared across the table at his mother. "What exactly *were* you thinking?"

His mother sniffed. "I need your help, son." She sent a glance of her own at Grace, as though she were weighing her words. "I—I need some time away."

"Why? Because now you can't handle raising your

daughter?" He shot Grace a knowing look. "Yep, looks like she's about the same age I was when you left Dad and me."

A tear pooled along the side of his mother's nose. "I'm a bad mother—I admit it." She leaned forward and dropped her voice to a frantic whisper. "That's why I need you to take her for a while."

"I can hear you, Mother." Grace huffed and stared out the window.

Kip felt the worst headache of his life coming on. He rubbed his eyes furiously. Just this morning he'd imagined having Ryan for a little brother. Now he had a flesh-and-blood sister—a sister his mother wanted to pawn off on him for who knew how long! He felt for the girl, he really did, but be responsible for her? They had to be kidding!

"I know this is a huge shock, but I got nobody else I can turn to." His mother's Texas drawl lilted sweet as honey off the comb. So sickeningly sweet his throat tingled. The whine came back into her voice. "I've been lookin' for you for weeks. I'd just about given up hope."

His stomach heaved. "It was you Tom Jacobs ran into at the ranch supply. You lied, made him believe you were one of my saddle customers."

She lowered her eyes. "I learned years ago not to tell people I was your mother, 'cause then nobody would tell me anything."

"Well, I know for a fact Tom didn't tell you, so how'd you find out?"

"Some folks at the ranch supply remembered where you used to live." His mother licked her lips. Her eyes darted sideways. "I sweet-talked your landlord into telling me where your mail was being forwarded."

General Delivery, Kingsley, North Carolina. And

knowing his mother, he wouldn't even venture a guess as to what that "sweet-talk" entailed.

Lord, Lord! Why this? Why now? Just when I thought I could trust You again!

Sheridan stepped from her Prius and struggled for a calm she didn't feel. Only a few cars dotted the Kingsley Station lot, but the one that caught her attention was Kip's white pickup, angling across two spaces as if he'd parked carelessly—not like him at all.

Then there was the rusted-out green Dodge parked next to Kip's pickup and bearing Texas plates.

Bracing herself, she strode into the restaurant. Her voice sounded high and stiff as she told the hostess she was meeting someone.

"Oh, that cowboy and his two lady friends? Right this way."

Two lady friends? Sheridan hurried after the hostess, already several steps ahead. Rounding a partition, she glimpsed Kip in a booth overlooking the tracks.

Across from him sat a seedy-looking woman with the ugliest bleach-blond hair Sheridan had ever seen. The hair might be different—blond, a little longer—but something about the woman evoked memories of Dell Finston. An acrid taste of peanut butter cookies rose in Sheridan's throat. She gulped air.

Then she noticed the girl next to the window. Just a kid, really, and looking like misery personified.

Who were these people?

She approached the table, her spine rigid. "Kip?"

He whipped his head around so fast she was afraid it would snap off his neck. "Sheridan."

"Am I interrupting?" Stupid question since clearly she was. But he'd told her to come.

Kip tried to get up but caught his thigh on the underside of the table. Cursing under his breath, he found his balance and stood between her and the women. His eyelids fluttered closed. He clawed a hand through his hair. "I didn't want you to find out like this."

Now she wanted the truth more than ever, even though she feared it could mean the end of whatever had begun to grow between them in these few short weeks. She shifted her purse to her other shoulder. "Find out what?"

With an exhalation that seemed to come from the soles of his feet, Kip stepped to the side and extended a hand toward the booth. "Sheridan, this is my—my mother, Janine Lorimer Lawton." He swallowed. "And my sister, Grace."

Chapter Fifteen

A paralyzing numbness seeped through Sheridan's limbs. With effort she managed to lift the corners of her mouth into a semblance of a smile. "How do you do, Mrs. Lor—I mean, Lawton? I'm Sheridan Cross."

The woman sat tying a paper straw wrapper in knots. Her lips quivered. She flicked a nervous glance in Sheridan's direction.

Kip extended his arm and nodded toward the bench seat he'd just vacated. "Maybe you should sit down."

"Maybe I should." Sheridan slid into the booth, and Kip edged in beside her. Under the table he reached for her hand, his palm cold and clammy.

"Kip tells me he works for y'all?" Forced politeness brightened the woman's tone.

Even from across the table, Sheridan caught the fetid smell of stale tobacco. She squeezed Kip's hand to fight off the nausea that threatened. Dell Finston's image wavered in and out every time Sheridan looked at the woman.

Maybe Kip sensed what she felt, or maybe he just wanted to get this meeting over with. He fisted his other hand and pressed it into the table top. "My mo—" A strangled sound came from his throat. "Janine's come here looking for my help with Grace."

Mentally Sheridan did the math. Kip had mentioned he was thirty. If Grace was only around fifteen . . .

Kip appeared to notice her confusion. "Janine married a guy named Lawton a few years ago, but Grace is my full sister. She was born after—after Janine left. I never knew I had a sister until today."

The girl suddenly shifted, angry brown eyes drilling through her mother before she slanted a sneer at Kip. "Bet you're sorry as all get-out, too."

"That's not true. It's just . . ." Kip's fist trembled. He huffed a pained breath.

Sheridan's heart broke for him. She'd suspected all along that Kip had good reason for not wanting to talk about his family. But to find out so suddenly about a sister he never knew existed? Sheridan could only imagine his agony.

And one look at Grace spoke volumes. Her home life didn't appear to be any better than that of most of the kids in the group home. If Kip's mother had come seeking help for Grace . . .

"Mrs. Lawton, has Kip told you about the program we run at Cross Roads Farm?" She felt Kip stiffen beside her.

"Program?" Janine shifted her gaze between Kip and Sheridan. "What kind of program?"

"We're an accredited equine therapy center. We have classes for kids of all ages in horsemanship and riding."

"Equine therapy." The woman scratched her ear. "I've heard of that. I thought it was for handicapped kids."

"Some of our clients have disabilities. Others are . . ." Sheridan pressed her lips together and flicked a glance toward Grace. "Others are kids who've faced some trouble in their lives and need a safe place to heal."

"Sheridan." Kip's quiet tone held a sharp edge. He pressed her hand against his thigh.

Across the table, Kip's mother stared at Grace with a look Sheridan had come to recognize after years of working with the Cross Roads Farm clients and their families. It was the faintest glimmer of hope.

Grace glared back and wedged herself deeper into the corner. "Forget it, Mother. You're the one who needs therapy, not me."

Tears running down her cheeks, Mrs. Lorimer seized Kip's wrist. "Please, son, take her for a while, just till I get some . . . things . . . taken care of." Chin quivering, she leaned closer. "Please. You're the only one I can trust."

Kip wasn't completely sure how it happened, but somehow Grace ended up sitting next to him in the pickup, her battered suitcase tossed in the back and an envelope stuffed with scribbled permission forms on the seat between them. The only tears shed as they left the restaurant were his mother's. Whether from relief or genuine sorrow over saying goodbye to her daughter, Kip couldn't be sure. Maybe both.

Then Janine Lawton had hurried to her beat-up old Dodge and headed out of town. "I'll try to call you in a few days," was all she'd said. Didn't say when she'd be back, didn't even offer a phone number after he'd reluctantly given her his.

So what else was new? Janine was the type who'd always thought she'd find greener pastures on the other side of the next fence. More money. More glamour. More class. The love of a good man never provided quite enough to keep her satisfied. Country music entertainer Clyde Lawton was her fourth husband, if Kip hadn't lost count, but apparently they were splitsville now, too.

He shook his head to clear away the debris. Time to focus on the present and get his mind around the idea of taking Grace back to the farm with him. Which certainly hadn't been *his* idea.

Nope, it was all Sheridan. And her mom, of course. Sheridan had excused herself to make a phone call, then returned to the table to say everything was all worked out. Grace would stay in the main house with the Crosses.

He wondered how he would have handled things if Sheridan hadn't been there. Sent his mother and sister packing?

His breath snagged. No, he'd have figured out *something*. No denying that the desperation in his mother's eyes and the defiance in Grace's had penetrated his heart. Maybe he wasn't ready to forgive his mother, but for now he could only hope to make a difference in his sister's life for as long as he had this chance.

His thoughts took him down a road that only a month ago he'd never have traveled. He could see himself and Sheridan married, making a home together, maybe right down the road from Cross Roads Farm. And they'd get custody of Grace and make sure Janine never—

"She your girlfriend?"

Kip kept his eyes glued to the rear bumper of the red Prius in front of them. "Yeah, I guess she is." He glanced at his sister. "I hope you appreciate the chance she's taking, inviting you into their home."

"You afraid I'll rip them off?" Grace crossed her arms with a snort. "Like I care."

Kip rubbed his upper lip. This was going nowhere fast. The Cross Roads Farm sign came into view, and Kip slowed behind Sheridan to turn into the lane. He sensed Grace sitting up straighter. Her breath quickened.

He eased his foot off the accelerator and imagined the farm through Grace's eyes. Rolling pastures, contented horses, a freshly painted white rail fence around the main house. "Nice place, huh?"

She slumped again. "I've seen worse."

By the time he parked next to the caretaker's cottage, Sheridan and Mrs. Cross stood waiting nearby. Mrs. Cross wore her usual welcoming smile. Sheridan smiled, too, but more warily, like she couldn't quite believe she'd actually suggested this arrangement.

If he wasn't sure he loved her before, now he was certain. As he stepped from the pickup, his heart swelled until he could hardly catch a breath. He ached to take Sheridan aside, hold her in his arms, and thank her from the depths of his being, because he knew the level of trust it had taken for her to receive yet another stranger into her life.

Grace heaved herself out the passenger door with a groan. Hands stuffed into her jeans pockets, she stared at the dirt while Kip grabbed her suitcase out of the pickup bed.

Mrs. Cross hurried over and introduced herself. "We're so glad to have you here, Grace." She ran a fingertip along a loose strand of Grace's hair and then wrapped an arm around the girl's shoulder. "Come on inside. I imagine you'd enjoy a long, hot soak in the tub before dinner."

Kip followed them as far as the back porch, then handed

off the suitcase to Grace. As she and Mrs. Cross strolled inside, he pulled Sheridan to the other end of the porch. Planting his hips against the railing, he drew Sheridan close. Bone-deep tiredness suddenly swamped him. All he could do was murmur, "Thank you. Thank you."

"I'd do anything for you, Kip. Don't you know that by now?" Her arms crept up his back, one hand caressing his nape.

The sweet scent of her cologne made him weak with longing. A choking thickness clogged his throat. "I was so scared I'd have to leave the farm. Leave you."

She lifted her head from his chest and narrowed one eye. "Not on your life, cowboy."

"I'm sure glad you feel that way." A slow grin spread across his face and into his heart before he claimed those sweet, sweet lips and the woman they belonged to. God willing, he'd spend the rest of his days right here where he'd finally found home—in the arms of Sheridan Cross.

Between Nathan's moodiness and Grace's surliness, dinner proved a tense affair. Sheridan tried to follow her mother's lead and keep the cheery chatter flowing, and Kip—bless his heart—contributed more table conversation than Sheridan had heard out of him in all the time he'd been at the farm.

She could see how the day's events had drained him, so after a few more kisses on the twilit porch, she sent him off to the cottage. In the meantime, since Nathan currently occupied the downstairs guest room, Mom settled Grace into Nathan's bedroom across the hall from Sheridan's. Poor Grace had seemed as tired and shell-shocked as Kip, and no wonder—

meeting her brother for the very first time, then being packed off to stay with strangers. Sheridan prayed the girl would adjust quickly—most especially, that spending time with the horses would soothe her soul as it had for so many other children who'd passed through the gates of Cross Roads Farm.

Mom entered the kitchen, an overflowing laundry basket braced against her hip. An acrid odor preceded her. "Everything in that poor girl's suitcase reeked of smoke! I gave her one of Nathan's T-shirts to sleep in."

"Here, let me help." Together they loaded the washer, and Sheridan suggested adding a big scoop of baking soda to help eliminate the smells.

Back in the kitchen, Mom marched straight to the electric teakettle. "I could use a cup of chamomile. How about you?"

"Sounds perfect."

They carried their mugs to the darkened living room and sat hip to hip on the sofa, sipping their tea in pleasant silence. After a bit, Mom set her mug on the coffee table, tucked her legs under her, and slid one arm around Sheridan's back. "I love you, honey."

Sheridan touched her temple to her mother's. "Could you tell how much it meant to Kip that you invited Grace to stay with us?"

Mom kissed her forehead. "Yes, and I could tell how much it meant to *you*."

"I love him, Mom." There, she'd said it. Her heart lifted.

"I know. And I'm glad."

"If we hadn't brought Grace home, I don't think he would have stayed."

Mom straightened and reached for her mug. As she

sipped her tea, she eyed Sheridan over the rim. "Is that the only reason you wanted to bring her here?"

"Maybe that was part of it, but I also believe we can help Grace." Sheridan pressed her lips together in thought. "I admit, the idea scared me at first. I mean, we don't even know this girl—and neither does Kip." She shuddered. "And her mother—all I could think about was how much she reminded me of Dell Finston."

"She sounds like a woman with some serious issues—trusting her daughter to people she doesn't even know, without so much as a hint of where she's going or when she'll be back."

Mom's words lingered in the silent room for several long moments. Then the truth hit Sheridan like a thunderbolt. "Oh, Mom, she did the same thing to Kip."

Mom's forehead wrinkled. "Did what?"

"Left him. She walked out on Kip and his father a few months before Grace was born."

Mom pushed off the sofa. Cradling her mug, she stared out the window behind Sheridan's head. "No wonder it took Kip so long to trust us. There's still a hurting little boy inside him."

"And now he's supposed to care for his hurting little sister." Sheridan set her empty mug on the coffee table and stood beside her mother. She hugged Mom's arm. "Sometimes I forget how blessed I am that I grew up with two loving parents."

Sudden awareness jolted Kip awake the next morning. Yep, he really had a sister, and she really had come to stay with him. With the Crosses, actually, which for her sake was a whole trailer load better than what he could offer.

But, at least until Janine showed her face again, Kip was still responsible for the girl, and it scared him silly. He'd had trouble enough all these years looking out for himself, and not always doing such a good job at that.

Dawn peeked over the horizon by the time he'd pulled on his jeans and boots and scarfed down a bowl of shredded wheat. He pushed open the screen door and stepped into the misty morning—his favorite time of day. The main house remained dark, and Manuelo wouldn't arrive for another half hour, so for now he had the farm to himself. Birdsongs rang through the air like a serenade. A butterfly flitted past his nose and alighted on a zinnia in the flowerbed beside his stoop. Gentle rustling sounds came from the barn as the horses stirred.

And then another sound, like whimpering. Kip followed the sound to its source, somewhere in the shadows deep within the barn. The whimpering became muffled sobs, and they came from Sundown's stall.

Kip peered over the stall gate and saw Grace leaning into Sundown, her shoulders shaking with each shuddering breath. She wrapped her arms around the horse's neck as if she held on to a life preserver—which maybe, at this moment, was exactly what the gentle horse was.

Kip's throat clenched as memories swam to the surface. To the day he died, he'd never forget the pain of being left behind, he and his dad discarded like a pair of old boots.

Seeing Kip at the stall door, Sundown must have expected breakfast. The horse nickered and nudged Grace aside. When her eyes met Kip's, she breathed an indignant huff and swiped the tears from her blotchy face.

"What are you staring at? Never seen anybody cry

before?" Grace tugged at the oversized T-shirt that brushed her bare knees. At least she'd had the common sense to pull those scruffy brown boots on before coming out to the barn.

Kip unlatched the door and stepped through, pausing to stroke Sundown's muzzle. "Breakfast is coming, boy. Hold your horses." He bent down to check Sundown's hoof. "I know what it's like getting left behind, Grace. But I promise you'll be safe here. I'll do my best to take good care of you. And Mrs. Cross, she's—"

"He looks just like Duke."

Straightening, Kip realized she spoke of Sundown. "Is Duke your horse?"

A hiccup, a sniffle, and another sob tore from Grace's throat. "After Clyde threw us out, she said we couldn't afford to keep a horse. Now I've got nothing. No one!"

She stumbled toward Kip, and the next thing he knew, he was cradling her against his chest. One hand seemed to naturally find its way up to her head, and the other patted her back all on its own, like he'd been doing this brother thing all his life. Her wet, slobbery tears soaked through to his skin, but he held on tight. "You have me, Grace. You have me."

"We're short two volunteers today." Sheridan's mother strode over to the arena rail, where Sheridan was helping one of their Thursday-morning riders groom Gem for class.

"That's right, Zoe. Keep brushing down Gem's neck the same direction his hair grows." Keeping one eye on the girl, Sheridan scanned the arena and did a quick head count. "Who's missing?"

"Cheryl and Camy are having car trouble."

"Great. Our twin horse leaders." Sheridan kept her voice low so as not to panic Zoe, who tended to worry about everyone else.

"It's too late to call someone on the sub list." Mom checked the stirrup leathers on the English saddle balanced on the rail. "Kip can cover for one of the twins, but no one else out here today is a trained horse leader."

Sheridan glanced up to see Grace walking Sundown out of the barn. The old boy was finally off stall rest but not quite up to classes yet. Yesterday Kip had confided in Sheridan about Grace's tearful breakdown. He'd started letting Grace walk Sundown up and down the lane and around the property to give him a little exercise.

"Mom? How about asking Grace to fill in?"

Mom quirked her lips. "But she hasn't had volunteer training."

Coming up beside them, Zoe tossed the grooming brush into the tote. "Gem's ready for his saddle now."

"Sure, honey." Sheridan handed the girl a white fleece saddle pad and helped her center it on Gem's back. Lifting the saddle off the rail, she nudged her mother's elbow. "These are able-bodied kids, Mom. All Grace needs to do is be there in case the rider needs redirection. And from what I've seen, she has enough horse sense to handle it."

Mom waited until Sheridan had helped Zoe tighten the girth and then handed Sheridan Gem's bridle. "Yes, but does she have enough *common* sense?"

"Put her with Tina. She's our best rider."

"Good idea." Mom hurried out the arena gate to catch up with Grace.

And good luck convincing her to help.

On the other hand, Sheridan had been pleasantly

surprised to see how quickly Grace was accepting her new living arrangements—even more, the idea of spending time with her brother. Whatever happened in the barn yesterday morning, Grace and Kip seemed to be attached at the hip ever since. The only downside was that with his little sister shadowing Kip's every move, Sheridan had a hard time getting her man alone. The best she'd managed yesterday was to meet Kip on the porch after everyone else had gone to bed. And by then, they'd both been too exhausted to talk, so they simply snuggled on the swing.

Sheridan soon had Zoe mounted and ready to ride, and as the girl took her first laps around the arena, Sheridan looked over to see Grace standing next to Tina as the redheaded twelve-year-old prepared to mount Gigi. Grace didn't look exactly happy to be helping out, but by the time class was underway, she seemed to relax, maybe even show off a little as she reminded Tina to keep her heels down and her chin up.

It's happening again, Dad—another troubled kid finding hope and healing. Sheridan swallowed the lump in her throat. She caught Kip's eye across the arena, nodded toward Grace, and winked. His grin was the only answer she needed.

When class ended and the last of the kids had left, Sheridan snagged her mother's arm on their way out of the barn. "Can you find something for Grace to do in the house for a while?"

"You'll owe me one." Mom winked and marched into the tack room, where Grace and Kip were still putting things away.

Seconds later, Mom and Grace stepped out. "I've been threatening to clean out Nathan's closet ever since he went off to college. Having you here gives me the perfect excuse."

Oh, boy. *Sorry, Nathan.*

Not! The packrat deserved this.

And Sheridan deserved some quality time with Kip. She sauntered into the tack room and let her gaze travel every inch of his muscled, blue-jeaned, Stetson-topped figure as he strained to shove a saddle onto the top tier of racks.

Her chest warmed. An easy grin slid across her face. "Hey, handsome. What's a nice cowboy like you doin' in a place like this?"

Kip turned and cocked his head. His lazy smile sent shivers down Sheridan's spine. "Why, howdy, ma'am. Why don't you just come on over here and find out?"

Chapter Sixteen

Kip breathed deeply through his nose, savoring the fresh herbal scent of Sheridan's shampoo. Her soft cap of waves felt like satin against his cheek. He pressed a kiss against the tender spot behind her ear and tasted the salty-sweetness of her skin.

She sighed and melted into his chest. "Thought I'd never get you alone again."

"I know the feeling." He locked one arm around her waist and with his free hand tilted her chin. Her lips parted slightly, inviting him. His pulse stammered.

He kissed her shyly at first, then hungrily, as if he could never get enough of her. His whole world narrowed to just this moment, and nothing else mattered except holding Sheridan in his arms.

Heart thudding, he drew back to gaze into her eyes. "You're dangerous, woman. A man could get used to this kind of thing and never get any work done around here."

Sheridan laced her fingers behind his neck. "Dangerous, huh? I think I like the sound of that."

"Sher, I—" Kip hauled in a breath and touched his

forehead to hers. "Maybe it's time we had that talk we never got around to."

She stepped back, her hands skimming down his arms. The sensation almost made him forget what he'd just said. "It's about your family, right? Kip, I think I can guess. You don't have to—"

"No. I do. Because I'm—" He was about to say it, admit it out loud, and he didn't care. Nothing had ever felt so right. "Because, Sheridan Cross, I'm crazy in love with you and you deserve to know it all."

She blinked. Smiled. Shivered. Then sighed. "Okay, but just so you know, there's not a thing on God's green earth that will change the fact that I'm crazy in love with you, too."

His heart leapfrogged his Adam's apple, and he was sorely tempted to forget the talk and just kiss her until either his lips fell off or the world ended. But good sense prevailed and he took Sheridan by the hand and led her out of the barn. Better to talk somewhere in plain sight so as to avoid either one of them getting distracted by . . . other things.

A tall, spreading oak stood at the corner of the Crosses' backyard, and beneath it sat a small wrought-iron table and two chairs. Kip pulled the chairs close enough that he could hold Sheridan's hand. A sultry breeze stirred the leaves above them.

"Okay, cowboy, I'm listening." Sheridan gently rocked in her chair. "Would it help if I tell you what I already know . . . or suspect?"

Kip's voice suddenly wouldn't cooperate, so he simply nodded. Leaning forward, he fixed his gaze on a beetle crawling through the grass between his boots.

"You said your mom left just before Grace came along."

"Yep."

"And since you don't seem to be on speaking terms with her, I'm guessing your parents didn't part as friends."

"Right again." Kip rubbed his eyes and sat up. "My dad was one tough cowboy, a champion bronc buster and bull rider in his heyday. And he could wrestle the meanest steer to the ground in three seconds flat."

"Three seconds. Is that good?"

"Good enough for the championship, nine times out of ten." Kip fingered the silver belt buckle he wore, a cherished memento from his dad. "But the rodeo life isn't all fame and glory. On the road most of the year, living out of a cramped trailer, unpredictable income, injuries that can sideline a man for months at a time."

Sheridan's breath escaped in a harsh sigh. "That's why your mother left him?"

"I don't know if he ever even knew about Grace, seein' as how Janine kept her a secret from me all these years. Part of me understands why she wouldn't want to raise another child, especially a girl, in that kind of life, but . . ." Kip fisted one hand. Try as he might, he couldn't bring himself to forgive his mother for the pain and heartbreak.

Bitterness heated Sheridan's words. "I don't care how hard her life was, marriage is a commitment. And besides, mothers just don't abandon their children like that."

Kip mashed his lips together and drew in a long, slow breath through his nostrils. He reached for Sheridan's hand. "She's tried to apologize over the years—when I'd even give her the time of day."

Sheridan lowered her voice. "Is your mother the reason you left Texas?"

"Exactly." While sparing her some of the uglier details, Kip explained how after he grew up, his mother would come looking for him every few years, usually in need of some cash to tide her over between husbands or to pay off a loan shark. Kip had had personal encounters with a couple of those creeps—or rather their fists. When a confrontation with an especially mean blood-sucker sent Kip to the ER for stitches, a concussion, and three cracked ribs, he'd decided enough was enough. "Last time she came looking for me, I told her to stay out of my life and shovel her own piles of manure."

Sheridan set her chair to rocking again. She tapped her fingernails against the black metal chair arm. "What do you think she's up to now, Kip—tracking you down, insisting you take Grace?"

"I don't even want to think about what kind of trouble she's gotten herself into this time."

"Well, whatever it is, you don't have to deal with it alone. You've got me now." Her gaze softened. "Always."

Strength flowed from her hand into his, and he tightened his grip, drinking up the love in her eyes and thanking the Lord above for sending Sheridan into his life.

The next few days went by without much excitement, which was fine with Sheridan. This summer had brought one surprise after another. Some good, some not so good . . . and some downright wonderful. Heaving a contented sigh, she stared through the wispy curtains covering Nathan's window, her gaze following Kip as he took Jet through his paces in the jump arena that Sunday evening. Grace watched from the fence rail, looking as enraptured as Sheridan felt.

"Are you going to play a word or not?" Nathan's

snappish tone zapped her like a paperclip poked into an electrical socket.

She focused on her rack of Scrabble tiles, but her mind wouldn't settle. Finally she stuck a *C* and an *A* in front of a *T*. "Cat. How many points is that?"

Nathan sneered and picked up a pencil. "Do I have to do *everything* for you? Sheesh."

Sheridan glared at her brother. "I will be so glad when you're finally out of that neck brace and back to your old self. You've been a bear lately."

"And how would you know? You spend all your time mooning over the know-it-all cowboy." Nathan slapped a *W, E, I,* and a *D* across the *R* at the top of RAZOR. "You forgot to draw two tiles."

She slid her hand into the little gray bag and fingered several of the cool squares before selecting two of them. An *M* and a *Q.* Great. "Why are you talking so mean about Kip?"

Nathan glanced toward the window, a slight quiver in his lower lip. "Sorry, just a little fed up with . . . stuff."

"It's Jet, isn't it?" Sheridan nudged her tile rack aside and rested her forearms on the table. "It's killing you that you're not the one out there riding him."

"If you're not going to play, then put the game away." Nathan skimmed a hand across the board, brushing the tiles onto the table.

"Nathan!"

"Just leave me alone, okay?" He shoved his chair back, only to wince in pain.

Sheridan sprang from her chair and darted around behind him. She set her hands on his shoulders, massaging with gentle but firm pressure. "Sit still, okay? Better?"

He answered with a grudging snort.

"You're acting like a spoiled brat, you know." When she felt the tension leave his muscles, she gave him a pat and plopped onto the side of the bed. "Come on, Nathan, you should be glad Kip can ride Jet like he needs to be ridden. That horse was a handful even for Dad."

"And, of course, I'm not *half* the rider Dad was."

"I didn't mean it like that."

"Sure you did. I'll never . . ." Nathan huffed and turned toward the window.

"Never what?"

"Nothing. Quit hovering and go be with your cowboy."

She'd like nothing better, but she hated leaving her brother in this state. Depressed didn't begin to describe Nathan's mood lately. He seemed more discouraged and angry with every passing day.

She helped her brother put away the Scrabble game and then planted a kiss on the top of his head before leaving him to his doldrums. As she started out the front door, Nathan's words echoed in her thoughts: *not half the rider Dad was.*

Nathan had always looked up to their father, always wanted to be just like him. And Jet was Dad's horse, his pride and joy. Trophies and ribbons weighed down the shelves in Dad's study. And now, with Dad gone, the fact that Nathan couldn't handle Jet must be eating a hole in his spirit, not to mention his manly pride.

Sheridan paused on the front porch steps to watch Kip take Jet over a double oxer jump. It suddenly occurred to her that Kip and Nathan were more alike than either of them realized, each determined in his own way to carry on his father's legacy. If only they could accept their individuality, believe in their own God-given strengths. If only they'd learn to trust God for their self-worth instead of feeling like they had something to prove.

Kip ended his ride with a successful jump at the Liverpool, then slowed Jet to a cool-down walk around the arena. On his next circuit, he glimpsed Sheridan walking up the lane, her sandals raising puffs of fine dust.

"Nice ride," she called. She rested a hand on the rail next to where Grace stood leaning against the fence.

"Just finishing up." Kip unbuckled his riding helmet and passed it down to Grace. "How was your Scrabble game?"

Sheridan's gaze shifted sideways. "We didn't finish."

Nathan must be in one of his moods again. Kip made a mental note to call Tom Jacobs again and see what they could work out about getting Ember delivered. He had yet to mention the plan to Sheridan or Mrs. Cross. And he sure wouldn't bring it up with Nathan until the time was right.

He kicked out of the stirrups and swung down off the horse. Taking the reins, he started for the gate. Grace held it open for him. "Can I lead Jet back to the barn?" she asked.

He chewed his lip. Jet was plenty worn down after their forty-five-minute ride, and Kip sure wouldn't mind trading riding gloves and leather reins for a pretty lady's soft hand in his. Exchanging the reins for his helmet, he handed off the horse to Grace. "He's all yours."

They ambled toward the barn, Grace at Jet's left and Kip on the right, between the big horse and Sheridan's bare toes. Downright pretty toes, he had to admit. He caught himself staring at those pink-painted nails and grinning.

With Grace's help he made short work of stowing Jet's

tack and giving the horse a quick rinse-off in the wash rack. After releasing Jet into his stall, he dropped a fresh flake of hay over the gate and then found Sheridan talking with Grace outside Sundown's stall.

Grace looked up at Kip's approach. "How soon before Sundown can be ridden again? He's not limping at all anymore."

The hopeful look in her eyes corkscrewed through Kip's heart. "The farrier will be back out tomorrow. We'll see what he says." When Grace rested her chin on the stall gate to watch Sundown munch on his hay, Kip tugged Sheridan beneath his arm and stole a kiss.

His sister glanced over her shoulder with a smirk. "I heard that."

"Heard what?" Sheridan's voice was all sugary innocence. She laid a hand against Kip's chest in a way that made his heart beat faster.

Grace rolled her eyes then made a big show of checking her watch—except she wasn't wearing one. "Will you *look* at the time. I'm late for a very important . . . needlepoint lesson or laundry folding or—I know! I can groom the dogs. Again!"

Kip could only chuckle as Grace bestowed a regal wave before jogging toward the house. "You think she's onto us?"

"You mean all the busy work we've come up with lately so we can be alone together?" Sheridan poked him in the ribs. "Yeah, I'd say she's onto us."

"Sure makes doin' this easier." Kip pulled her against him and enjoyed a long, lazy kiss.

Sheridan's hands crept up his chest, and she gently pushed him away. A troubled look clouded her eyes.

"You still thinking about Nathan?"

She pushed out her lower lip. "It's clearer than ever how jealous he is of how easily you handle Jet."

"I suspected as much." Kip drew her out into the dusky evening. A few stars already shone overhead, flickering through wispy mare's-tail clouds. The frogs down by the creek had picked up a lively tune, a sure sign rain was on the way.

Sheridan leaned into his shoulder as they strolled along the lane. Kip knew he must smell like the sweaty cowboy he was, but she didn't seem to care. Or maybe the breeze carried his aroma downwind.

"I'm worried about Nathan," she said. "I'm starting to think this started long before his accident. I think he's still mourning our dad. And now that he can't ride Jet, it's like he thinks he's letting Daddy down somehow."

They arrived at Kip's pickup. He unlatched the tailgate and lowered it, then scooted onto the edge and helped Sheridan up beside him. She crossed her ankles and kicked her sandaled feet in a leisurely rhythm.

Kip laced his fingers through hers. "I think the best thing for Nathan is to find him the right horse. And I, uh, I've been working on that."

Sheridan looked at him with a curious smile. "What exactly are you up to, Mr. Lorimer?"

"I've talked to my friend back in Texas—Tom Jacobs. He has a horse we both think would be ideal for Nathan." Kip pulled in a long breath and blew it out in a whoosh. "I'm afraid he'll lose his confidence entirely if we don't get him back on a horse—the *right* horse—as soon as he's able."

"Hopefully that'll be soon. I'm praying for anything that will give me back my typically fun-loving if annoying little brother."

"I'll give Tom another call tonight and see what we can do about getting that horse delivered." Kip brushed Sheridan's knuckles with a kiss.

"We can't make Nathan feel like a charity case, though." Sheridan laid her head against Kip's shoulder, the sweet, clean scent of her hair filling his senses.

Lost in the moment, he almost forgot what they were talking about. "I'll think of something, maybe find a way to make it Nathan's idea."

"Perfect." Thunder rumbled in the distance. One by one, the stars winked out as the clouds thickened. Sheridan looked skyward with a groan. "Looks like we're in for another fun night with Jet."

Chapter Seventeen

Feeling the first sprinkles of rain, Sheridan decided she'd better scamper back to the house before she got drenched. "Let me change into my paddock boots and grab a slicker, and I'll meet you at the barn. Maybe we can keep Jet calm enough to avoid a full-blown panic attack."

Kip helped her off the tailgate and slammed it shut. "I can handle him. No sense both of us running around in the storm."

"Did you already forget what happened last time?" Grinning, Sheridan peered down at Kip's feet. "At least you've got your boots on tonight, cowboy."

One side of his mouth quirked, and he tugged her close. "Once the storm passes, you might oughta check my foot again. I'm not so certain that sliver's completely out."

"Oh, really? Then maybe I should bring Mom's darning needle and a big ol' bottle of rubbing alcohol."

Kip shoved her away. "That's okay! A little gangrene never hurt anybody."

A thunder clap sent Sheridan straight into Kip's arms.

His rippling laughter was the most beautiful sound she'd ever heard.

His kiss was about the sweetest thing she'd ever tasted.

It took every last ounce of will power to tear herself away. "Barn. Now." She aimed a schoolteacher finger toward the building. "I'll catch up with you as soon as I change."

"Yes, ma'am!" Kip clicked his heels and saluted.

Sheridan bounded onto the porch seconds before the sky opened up. She sent up a quick prayer that Kip could settle Jet before the poor horse went ballistic.

She found Mom, Nathan, and Grace in the kitchen and both dogs cowering under the table. Lightning strobed through the windows. Xena whimpered and covered her face with one paw. Another flash, another thunderous explosion, and the power went out.

"Great." Mom fumbled through a drawer and snapped on a flashlight. The yellow beam danced across the walls and lit up anxious faces.

Nathan started for the door. "I should be out there with Jet."

Mom seized his wrist. "You'll just get yourself hurt again and—"

"Would you stop babying me!" Nathan shook off her hand. "Jet's *my* horse now. I'm the one who should be taking care of him."

Sheridan blocked Nathan's way. "Kip's with him. He'll be fine. I just came in to get my boots and a slicker, and then I'll go out and—"

"You'll do no such thing!" Mom glanced between Sheridan and the window as another brilliant flash lit up the room. "With all this lightning, it's too dangerous. That fool horse has been a handful since day one. If he kicks down his stall door again and takes off for Timbuktu, so be it. I just hope Kip has sense enough to stay out of his way."

Sheridan knew her mother was right, but the thought of Kip out there alone with Jet tied her stomach in knots. The next burst of lightning revealed Nathan's angry frown. He heaved a rough sigh and trudged to the window.

Sheridan took a calming breath of her own and finger-combed her damp hair. She felt useless and frustrated, trapped inside when all she wanted was to make sure the man she loved was safe. Maybe she'd change into jeans and boots anyway so she'd be ready as soon as the storm let up.

As she grabbed another flashlight and started for the hallway, a soft sob caught her attention. She found Grace huddled on the floor, her knees drawn up. Beau had crept up to her side and buried his nose in her lap. The girl stroked the dog's head with one hand and brushed tears from her cheek with the other.

Sheridan knelt beside her. "What's wrong, Grace? Are you scared?"

"Is Kip gonna be okay?"

Thunder boomed, and they both jumped.

Catching her breath, Sheridan smoothed a loose strand of Grace's hair off her forehead. "Your brother's the calmest, most sensible man I know. And the best horseman, too," she added in a whisper.

"But if something happened—" Grace gulped back tears.

"Kip will be fine, honey, I promise." Sheridan wasn't sure whom she was trying harder to convince—Grace, or herself.

"You'll be fine, boy, I promise." Kip had haltered the trembling black horse and started walking him up and down the barn aisle about the time the electricity went out. The battery-powered emergency lights kicked on almost immediately, bathing the barn in a soothing purplish glow. Kip maintained a gentle prattle while he kept Jet moving, hoping to distract the horse from the pounding rain and cracks of thunder. Mostly it was working—that, plus a hefty dose of a calming herbal tincture from the equine emergency kit. A bite of carrot every now and then seemed to help, too.

Finally the rain subsided and the last rumbles of thunder sounded far off to the south. Jet blew out a breath that set his nostrils aquiver. The tension left his ears and neck, and he nosed Kip's hand in search of another carrot.

Kip chuckled and fished a carrot out of his pocket. "Here ya go, boy. You've earned it."

As the horse munched, Kip returned him to his stall and closed the gate. He turned to see Sheridan, Nathan, and Grace coming through the door.

Nathan marched straight to Jet's stall. "Hey, fella. Glad to see you don't look any worse for wear."

"He did fine." Behind Nathan's back, Kip shot Sheridan a praise-the-Lord grin.

Grace rushed forward and hugged Kip's arm. "I was worried about you. Nathan said Jet gets crazy in a storm."

"Knowing what to expect is half the battle." With his free hand, he reached up to tweak Grace's chin.

Sheridan ambled over, a smug smile creasing her lips. "Nice work, cowboy. Guess you didn't need any help after all."

With a glance in Nathan's direction, Kip motioned

Sheridan and Grace toward the door. "This might be as good a time as any for Nathan and me to have that talk."

"Oh . . . right." Sheridan reached for Grace's hand. "We'll just go check on the other horses." Her eyes spoke encouragement as she wiggled her fingers at him and turned to go.

Hands stuffed into his back pockets, Kip drew up beside Nathan, who stood at Jet's stall door watching the horse tear off bites of hay. "Jet is a fine, fine horse," Kip said softly. "A real champion."

"For my dad, maybe." A sigh raked through Nathan. "And you."

"Remember, I was practically born on the back of a horse. Grew up with 'em, rode 'em, trained 'em, got bucked off and got right back on more times than I care to count."

"Sounds about like my dad. He lived and breathed horses." Nathan strode across the aisle and leaned against the opposite wall. "As a kid I wasn't that into riding. I'd rather play baseball or soccer than take boring old riding lessons."

"How'd your dad feel about that?"

A thoughtful look twisted Nathan's mouth. He chuckled softly. "He just wanted me to have fun, do whatever made me happy. And the funny thing is, the more freedom he gave me, the more I wanted to make him proud."

Kip broke eye contact before Nathan could notice the sudden longing his words aroused. But it was no use dwelling on regrets. Right now he needed to help Nathan face his own truths. He scoured his brain for the right words.

"Nathan, I'm real sorry I never had a chance to know your dad. But over the summer I've gotten to know you and your family pretty well. I'd even go so far as to say you and I have become friends." Kip paused while Nathan nodded in agreement. "So do you trust me as your friend?"

Again, Nathan nodded. A crooked grin skewed his lips. "You think I'd let you near my sister if I *didn't* trust you?"

The teasing remark bled away some of the tension. Kip sidled over and leaned against the wall next to Nathan. "Then, as your friend talkin', I've learned the hard way that there's more to be proud of in admitting your limitations than in trying to prove you can do what you know good and well you can't."

Nathan cocked an eyebrow. "I *think* I understood that."

"Good, because I sure as all get-out don't think I can repeat it."

Nathan returned to Jet's stall door. His shoulders slumped as he gazed at the horse. "Fine. I admit it. Jet was my dad's horse and I'll never be able to ride him like Dad did." Because of the neck brace, he had to turn his whole body to glare at Kip. "There. You satisfied?"

"The question is, are *you*?" Kip strode across the aisle until he stood nose to nose with Nathan. "You can give up right now, never ride another horse as long as you live. Or you can start fresh on a mount that'll challenge your skills and grow your confidence without scaring you half to death every time you get on his back. You up for that?"

Nathan swallowed. "You gonna be around to teach me?"

Kip's glance flicked toward the barn door. Every now and then snatches of conversation between Sheridan and Grace drifted from the big barn. He pictured Sheridan with her arm around Grace, being a friend, being a sister. He pictured staying right here at Cross Roads Farm for the rest of his days. Making a home here. Making a family here. The thought alone sent a warm, cozy feeling through his veins, like hot cocoa on a cold night, or the heat of early-spring sunshine on his back when the wind blew chill.

He breathed in long and let it out slowly. "Yeah," he said. "I plan to be around a good long while."

"What? You're in Kingsley?" Kip moved his cell phone to his other ear and turned down the burner under his grilled cheese sandwich before he burnt it to a cinder.

Tom Jacobs's booming laughter pounded against Kip's eardrum. "Sittin' here enjoying a big ol' glass of Southern sweet tea. Got me a handsome little bay gelding in the trailer just waiting to see his new home."

"You brought Ember?" Kip slid his sandwich onto a plate and carried it to the table. "Why didn't you let me know you were coming?"

"Figured I'd surprise you. Needed a little vacation, and North Carolina seemed like as good a place as any. You gonna give me directions, or am I gonna have to order another platter of Carolina fried chicken and gravy?"

Kip chuckled. "That stuff'll give you a heart attack, Tom. Forget the fried chicken and get your sorry self out here to the farm right now." Remembering last night's rain would have flooded the low water crossing, Kip directed Tom the long way around. "I'll be watching for you at the barn."

Leave it to Tom to decide on his own to trek to North Carolina and personally deliver Ember. Kip wolfed down his sandwich and hurried out to the barn to find Manuelo. "Let's get a stall ready. We got a horse coming."

Manuelo pushed up from the hay bale where he'd been having lunch. "*Señora* Cross did not say anything."

"She didn't know. *I* didn't know!" Kip pushed back his Stetson and scratched his head. "We'd better use one of the empty stalls in Jet's barn. If you'll get some shavings, I'll set up feed and water pails."

Between the two of them, they quickly readied a stall for Ember. Now the trick would be explaining the horse's surprise arrival to the Crosses. Especially Nathan. After the storm last night, figuring they still had some time, Kip had hoped only to get Nathan *thinking* about the idea of a more suitable horse.

Kip glanced at his watch. And right about now that horse should be less than ten minutes away. *Oh, Lord, let this plan work, because it's too late to turn back now!*

Much as she'd come to dread the start of a new school year, Sheridan had decided this morning she'd better get serious about preparing. Sitting at the kitchen table with her laptop, she reviewed some of the notes she'd taken during the teacher enrichment class.

At the sound of tires on gravel, she looked up. "Mom? Are you expecting someone?"

"Not that I know of." Her mother rinsed the last plate from their noontime meal and set it in the dishwasher.

About that time, Xena and Beau stirred from their naps on the back porch and raised a chorus of barks. Sheridan rose and went to the window. "It's a fancy dually pickup pulling a gooseneck horse trailer."

"What on earth?" Drying her hands on a dishtowel, Mom joined Sheridan at the window.

"Oh, my, I think I know!" Sheridan danced a little jig and squeezed her mother's hands.

Mom grasped Sheridan's forearms and forced her to stand still. "All right, young lady, spill the beans."

"I'm pretty sure it's Kip's friend Tom Jacobs, the man we called for references."

"And he's *here*? With a horse trailer?" They both turned back to the window.

By now, Beau and Xena were giving the visitor their usual friendly greeting. Kip shooed the dogs off to the side as the big man opened the trailer doors and lowered the ramp. Seconds later they backed a sleek bay horse out of the trailer.

"Wow! He's *gorgeous*!" Grace swept through the kitchen and burst out the door without bothering to close it behind her.

"What's all the commotion?" Nathan stepped up beside Sheridan, then froze, his eyebrows stretching practically to his hairline as he gazed out the window.

Sheridan slid her arm around her brother's waist. "Um, Nathan, I think that's your new horse."

"My new—but when—" He gulped. "Are you sure?"

"Why don't we go find out?"

Sheridan followed her mother and Nathan across the yard, her heart pounding with excitement for her brother. As they neared the horse trailer, Mom lifted a hand in greeting. "Hello and welcome!"

"Tom Jacobs, ma'am." The broad-shouldered man handed off the horse's lead rope to Kip and moseyed over— yes, *moseyed* was the only way to describe it—to accept Mom's handshake. "A pleasure to make your acquaintance."

"Linda Cross. Kip speaks so highly of you, Mr. Jacobs."

He gave a rumbling laugh. "*Mr.* Jacobs was my pa. I'd be much obliged if you'd call me Tom."

"Then you must call me Linda." She still hadn't released the man's hand.

Drawing alongside her mother, Sheridan did a double-take. She couldn't remember the last time she'd seen her mother blush so becomingly. She cast Kip a wide-eyed stare.

He sent back a crooked grin and shrugged as he guided the horse closer to Nathan. "Didn't mean to spring this on you, but I've been workin' on finding you just the right horse. Nathan, meet Ember. I think you're gonna like him a lot."

"He's . . . beautiful." Nathan stretched out his hand, and Ember nosed his palm.

Mom starry-eyed over Tom Jacobs, Nathan starry-eyed over Ember, Grace starry-eyed over the horse *and* her amazing big brother . . .

Feeling a little starry-eyed herself, Sheridan drew away, content to simply enjoy this mutual admiration society. Xena and Beau, apparently jealous of the attention everyone else was getting, pranced up to her with wagging tails. Kneeling between them, Sheridan wrapped her arms around their necks and nuzzled their hairy faces. Life had never seemed so sweet.

Chapter Eighteen

Could life get any sweeter? In the cool of the evening, Kip held Sheridan's hand on the porch swing, while Tom and Mrs. Cross sat in wicker chairs sipping iced tea and chattering like a couple of teenagers on their first date. Grace and the dogs played a lively game of fetch on the lawn, and Nathan had walked out to the barn to get better acquainted with Ember.

"I still can't get over your friend coming all this way on a whim." Sheridan toyed with Kip's fingertips, sending icy-hot tingles up his arm.

Kip whispered out a slow breath and glanced in Tom's direction. "Looks like he and your mom are hittin' it off real well."

"*Real* well." Sheridan snuggled closer against Kip's side. "If I didn't know better, I'd think my mom was flirting." A shaky sigh slipped between her lips. "I never really thought about Mom meeting someone new after Dad died. It feels . . . weird. But also kind of nice."

"She couldn't find a nicer guy anywhere on God's green earth." Kip drew Sheridan beneath his arm and set the swing in motion. Peace like he'd never known washed over him like the waves off Galveston Island. Warm, constant, soothing.

The phone in his jeans pocket rang, startling him. Not that many people had his new number, and most of those folks sat right here on this porch. He shifted to tug out his cell phone and checked the caller ID. Unknown. Probably a wrong number.

Or Janine.

He shot Sheridan an uneasy frown as he answered the call.

"Kip? It's Mama."

His stomach sank to his boot heels. He pushed off the swing and strode to the other end of the porch. "Where are you?"

"Not far. How's Grace?"

"Grace is fine." He gazed across the backyard, where Grace rolled in the grass wrestling with Beau and Xena. Her happy laughter sang on the evening air.

"And you, son?" A nervous gulp. "You all right with . . . with everything?"

He pivoted and palmed his forehead. "*Everything?* As in the fact that you've lassoed me into your problems again? As in the fact that you kept my sister a secret from me all these years? As in the fact that you're off who-knows-where doin' who-knows-what and leavin' both me and Grace to wonder what happens next?"

"It's not like that, son—"

"Do *not* call me 'son.' You gave up that right sixteen years ago." A quick glance over his shoulder caught concerned looks from Mrs. Cross and Tom. Sheridan still sat on the swing, arms locked across her chest and her lips pressed into a worried frown.

"I know I did you wrong, and I'll hate myself for it till the day I die." Janine sniffed then coughed deep, hard, and long, like she was choking out a lung.

A new fear seized Kip's gut. He pressed the phone against his ear. "Are you sick? Is *that* what this is about?"

"No, it's—" Janine cleared her throat. "I smoke too much, that's all. I'm tryin' to quit. I promise, soon as I see to some stuff, I'll be back for Grace."

"How much longer?" Except Kip was feeling less and less inclined to return Grace to her care.

A pause. "I can't say for sure."

Grace now stood on the other side of the porch rail staring at Kip. The questioning look in her eyes told him she'd guessed who was on the line. Kip forced a smile, hoping she'd read an "all is well" into his expression. He wished he could convince himself.

"Listen, son—Kip—I gotta go. I know you're takin' good care of Grace. Tell her I love her."

"Janine?" *Mama?* But the line went dead.

Kip gazed into the dusky twilight and drew in several slow breaths. The air carried the sweet scent of a honeysuckle vine, but Kip's nostrils still burned with the memory of tobacco smoke and alcohol on his mother's breath the day she said she "just needed a little vacation" and never came back.

Sheridan met Kip near the porch steps. Her stomach clenched at the tortured look in his eyes. "Are you okay?"

"Fine." The grim line of his mouth gave a different answer.

"Was that your—was that Janine?"

Kip nodded. He drew a hand down his face and managed a wan smile. "You mind if I call it a night? I'm feelin' kinda wrung out."

It was barely past eight. The last rays of sun still winked through the tree line at the far edge of the horizon. Even so, Sheridan recognized the fatigue in Kip's eyes—a tiredness of the spirit. "Sure. I understand."

They'd already arranged for Tom Jacobs to park his rig next to the barn—a deluxe trailer with full living quarters and hookups, unlike the makeshift trailer/camper setup Kip had arrived with. Kip paused to thank Sheridan's mother for the evening meal and told Tom he'd see him in the morning.

Tom stood. "Ever'thing all right, son?"

Kip nodded toward Grace, still watching from the lawn. "Need to talk to my sister about a couple things. Then I'm plannin' on getting some shuteye."

Except Sheridan felt certain sleep would be a long time coming for Kip. She squeezed his arm and accepted his quick kiss on the cheek before he trudged down the porch steps. Draping an arm around Grace's shoulders, he walked with her out to the barn. Their talks always seemed to go better with the horses nearby.

"That boy's bothered about something or my name isn't Jacobs." The big man huffed and plopped into his chair.

Sheridan sank into a nearby chair with a groan. "This whole thing with Grace and their mother—I wish I knew how to help."

"Bad blood there. Always suspected as much."

Sheridan's mother reached for the tea pitcher to refill Tom's glass. "I sensed right away that he had a lot of healing to do. Seemed he'd been making real progress, too, until his mother showed up."

"I know for a fact his time here has been a blessing." Tom gave Sheridan's mother a quick grin before winking at Sheridan. "Yes, indeed, a true blessing."

At least the gathering dusk hid the blush that stung Sheridan's cheeks. She looked across the yard to see Grace ambling their way. Behind her, Kip lifted one hand in a tired wave before disappearing into the cottage. Grace joined them on the porch with a resigned smile. She sank onto the top step and leaned against the baluster.

Her voice low and tender, Sheridan's mother asked, "Any news from your mom, honey?"

"I guess she's not done with her business yet." Grace made a rude sound through her nose, but her next words came out on a shaky breath. "Which is fine with me. She can stay away forever as far as I'm concerned."

Sheridan rose and joined Grace on the step. "Whatever she's done, however many ways she's failed as a mother, she still loves you. I could see it in her eyes the day we first met."

"Kip told me the same thing." Grace's mouth skewed. She sniffed and swiped the back of her hand beneath her nose. "Except none of y'all have to live with her. Kip doesn't know how lucky he is. If you ask me, he got the best deal."

"Lucky?" Sheridan shifted to face the sulking teen. "To grow up believing his mother didn't want him? Have you even tried to imagine how hard it must have been for Kip to be left behind?"

Grace bent low to break off a blade of grass. She ran it between her fingers. "I didn't even know I had a big brother until this summer."

Sheridan touched Grace's shoulder. "Did she ever explain why she didn't tell you?"

"Just that Kip was Daddy's boy and I was her girl, and that's the way it had to be." She sighed. "Mom said they fought a lot before I came along. Mom wanted more out of life, but Daddy wouldn't give up the rodeo, even for her."

Sheridan guessed this was only half the story. She suspected there wasn't a man alive who could give a self-centered woman like Janine Lorimer Lawton the life she really wanted.

After an early breakfast with Tom Tuesday morning, Kip hurried over to the house for his usual duties helping Nathan shower, shave, and dress. He felt like an idiot for skipping out last night without asking if Nathan needed him for anything.

Mrs. Cross met him at the kitchen door. "You won't believe this, Kip. He's already out with Ember." Her cheeks crinkled in a happy grin. "I think he even slept in his clothes last night. One less hindrance for getting out to the barn in a hurry."

Kip lifted off his Stetson and rubbed his forehead with the back of his hand. He couldn't resist a satisfied chuckle. "Guess I'll go find him in the barn then."

"Kip." Before he realized what was happening, Mrs. Cross drew him into a motherly hug. "Thank you. From the bottom of my heart."

For a second or two he didn't quite know what to do with his arms, but finally he let them settle around Mrs. Cross's shoulders. She felt strong and soft and solid, all at the same time, the way a mother should feel. He closed his eyes and tried to picture Janine hugging him like this.

Then, from deep down in his memory, the pictures

came: A bandage on a scraped knee. A warm, soapy washcloth soothing a dirty face. He could almost remember the feeling of being comforted, cared for, loved.

Almost.

With three quick pats on his back, Mrs. Cross released him. She brushed something wet off her cheek. "Have you and Tom had breakfast? I can whip up some blueberry buckwheat pancakes."

"We were both up at the crack of dawn. I fixed us some scrambled eggs and—"

Footsteps sounded on the porch behind Kip. A firm hand clamped down on his shoulder. "Nothin' against your cooking, son, but what kind of a gentleman would I be if I turned down a lady's breakfast invitation?"

A girlish smile brightened Mrs. Cross's face. "Then get yourself right on into my kitchen, Mr. Jacobs, and sit yourself down while I heat up the griddle."

"You're *not* startin' that 'Mr. Jacobs' business again, are you?" Tom laughed and offered Mrs. Cross his arm.

Kip could only shake his head in wonder. What was it about Cross Roads Farm that stirred a lonely man's hankerin' for romance?

Or maybe it wasn't the farm but the pretty women who ran it.

Mrs. Cross paused in the doorway and glanced over her shoulder at Kip. "Will you join us?"

"No, thanks. Better see to the horses." Although he wondered if he should stick around to chaperone. "We got kids coming in a bit, in case you forgot."

When Mrs. Cross promised she'd be out in plenty of time to get set up for class, he tipped his hat and headed out to the barn.

Grace found him a short time later and pestered him to

give her a job. He assigned her the task of walking horses out to their designated pastures while he and Manuelo mucked out stalls.

Nathan wandered in from the small barn and leaned on the open stall door where Kip worked. "Wish I could help with that."

Kip heaved a forkful of manure and soiled shavings into the cart parked just outside the stall. "I'm sure you're missin' this dee-lightful experience like a bad bellyache."

Nathan heaved a sigh. "Till I practically broke my neck, I never realized half the stuff I'd miss doing."

"Nothin' like a brick up the side of the head to wake us up, huh?" Kip leaned on his pitchfork and studied the area at his feet. He'd had a few "bricks" of his own this summer, which might explain why he felt like he was lost in a fog most days. Couldn't be he was dazed by the gleam in a certain pretty lady's crystal-blue eyes, could it?

Nathan moseyed around the stall door and toed the wheel of the manure cart. "So . . . is Mr. Jacobs selling me Ember? Because I'm not trading Jet for him. Even if I never ride Jet again, I couldn't part with him."

"Not expecting you to. Tom hasn't talked money yet, but I know he'll be more than fair." Kip scooped up another forkful of manure. "About Jet . . . if he stayed right here at the farm, would you be interested in selling him to me?"

"Don't know about that." Nathan rubbed his jaw. "However, I might seriously consider giving you Jet as a wedding present."

A sucker punch to the breadbasket couldn't have hit Kip any harder. "We—I mean—that hasn't even been—"

"Discussed? Maybe not. But it's pretty clear that's the direction things are headed." Nathan ambled toward the barn door, where he paused and looked toward the main house. Then he chuckled to himself. "First Sheridan, now my mom. Must be something about a cowboy."

Sheridan lifted the electric teakettle and poured hot water over a Lady Grey teabag. "How long are you planning to stay in North Carolina, Mr. Jacobs?"

"Haven't decided." The tall Texan angled his chair away from the table and took a sip of his coffee. "Haven't had a real vacation since before my sweet wife of twenty-three years passed away five years ago. We used to take a couple of horses on a road trip every year—visit new parts of the country, find new trails to ride together." His gaze mellowed. "Jean would have loved North Carolina."

Sheridan's mother rose to refill Tom's mug. "You're welcome to stay at the farm as long as you like. We have a few trails around here you might enjoy."

"Is that an invitation to go riding with you?" He looked up at her with a boyish grin.

"Anytime."

Sheridan decided she'd better escape the kitchen before the violin serenade started. Leaving her mother and Tom to their coffee and conversation, she carried her mug of tea out the back door.

As she started for the barn, she saw Nathan ambling her way. "Hey, bro. You're up mighty early."

"Just visiting Ember." He wiggled his eyebrows at her. "And wheelin' and dealin' with Kip."

"Huh?"

"Never mind." Looking like the cat who swallowed a

whole flock of prize canaries, he brushed past her and headed to the house.

Brothers. Giving her head a brisk shake, Sheridan strode into the barn. The lemony fragrance of her tea mingled with the scent of fresh shavings. "Kip? You in here?"

No answer. A striped barn cat leapt from a crossbeam overhead and wove between Sheridan's legs. She bent down to scratch the cat behind its ears. With the horses all out to pasture, the barn stood in eerie silence. "Manuelo? Anybody?"

Still nothing.

Sheridan's skin crawled. Feeling a breath of air on the back of her neck, she spun around and came face to face with—

Nothing.

She ground her teeth together. Surely she ought to be over this paranoia by now. Or maybe she never would be, at least not completely.

"Sher?"

She whirled around again, this time splashing hot tea across her hand. Seeing Kip at the other end of the barn, she whooshed out a relieved sigh. "Where were you? Did you hear me call?"

"I was looking for something in the small barn's storage room." He strode toward her, his forehead creased beneath his hat brim. "You okay?"

"I just . . . worried when I didn't find you right away." She set her mug on a tack trunk and wiped her damp hand against her jeans. An embarrassed laugh caught in her throat.

Kip drew her close and warmed her lips with a kiss that tasted like wintergreen. "You want to help me get ready for class?"

"That's what I'm here for." She grinned. "Among other things."

While they organized grooming tools in the tack room, Sheridan ventured the question that had plagued her since last night. "Kip, I know your mother's phone call upset you. I wish you'd tell me about it."

He ran his thumb across the bristles of a stiff brush. "Like I said last night, she's still taking care of stuff. No idea what."

"But you must have a guess. A gut feeling." Sheridan shook some dirt out of an empty plastic pail before dropping in a curry and hoof pick.

"Money trouble, drinking, drugs—hard tellin'." He said it so matter-of-factly that it sent a chill up Sheridan's arms.

"Does she have a history of addiction?"

"I've had my suspicions. When she left my dad, she started hanging with musicians and roadies. Don't know why she thought their life was any more stable than a rodeo rider's. More glamorous, maybe. Cleaner." Kip examined a brush. "Janine never much cared for dirt."

"But to come looking for you all the way from Texas . . ." Sheridan tossed a bent hoof pick into the trashcan. "Why now? And why leave Grace? It makes me wonder if she's planning on coming back."

Kip froze and stared at her, but she could tell he wasn't really seeing her. He pulled in a noisy breath through his nostrils and then released it in a huff. He dropped the brush and dusted his hands on his jeans. "Can you finish this up? I gotta make a phone call."

"Kip—?"

But he was out the door and gone before the name left her lips.

Chapter Nineteen

Kip slapped his cell phone against his thigh with a grunt. Janine had never given him or Grace a number where she could be reached, and the Caller ID from last night registered unknown.

He paced in front of his kitchen sink, unable to escape the sinking feeling that his mother never intended to come back for Grace. On the one hand—at least for Grace's sake—maybe that wasn't such a bad thing. On the other . . . what did Kip know about raising a teenager? Even more pressing, what legal steps would he have to take to be appointed Grace's permanent guardian?

Don't jump the gun here, fella.

He needed to talk to Grace, to find out if she remembered anything more about what her mother had said before she took off.

He didn't have to wait long. Glancing out the front window, he spied his sister strolling toward the barn. He yanked open the door. "Hey, Grace. Come inside for a minute."

Grace drew up short with a confused look. "Mrs. Cross told me to help y'all in the barn. You done already?"

"Close enough." He held the door for her and motioned her toward the faded plaid sofa. Curling his hat brim, he lowered himself onto the ottoman. "Thought maybe we oughta talk some more about your mom."

Grace rolled her eyes and sank into the sofa cushions. "I'm plumb tired of talking about that woman, and I'd just as soon never see her again as long as I live."

"Be that as it may . . ." Kip laid his hat on the end table and then picked it up again. "I need to know, Grace. Did something happen back in Texas? Do you have any idea why your mom needed me to look after you for a while?"

Grace picked at a hangnail. "She's been weird ever since Clyde kicked us out."

"How long ago was that?"

"It was right after Christmas." Grace glared. "Mom ruins *everything*. Clyde was the best thing that ever happened to us. He's the one who got me Duke."

"Why'd they split?"

"'Cause she wanted to party and Clyde didn't. Said he'd done his time playin' honky-tonks and dance halls and wanted us to settle down and be a family." She sniffled. "She coulda left me with Clyde, but no. *Somebody* had to be around to clean up her messes when she came home dead drunk at four in the morning."

Kip clawed a hand through his hair. "Grace, I'm so sorry she did that to you. I wish you'd told me this right away."

"What difference would it make?" Grace shrugged. "Not like you can fix the past. Anyway, I'd just as soon forget the whole thing. I'm plenty happy right where I am."

"And I'm glad to have you here. But—" A sharp breath burst from Kip's lungs. "It's not that simple, Grace."

"Sure it is." She pushed off the sofa and marched to the door. One hand on the knob, she flung Kip an airy smile over her shoulder. "Next time Mom calls, you tell her to keep on goin' and never come back."

"Grace—"

But she slammed the door behind her before he had a chance to tell her that was exactly what he feared most.

Holding Lady's lead rope, Sheridan stared across the arena to where Kip stood working with Ryan and Gem. Kip was clearly preoccupied with something. Everything in his posture, everything in his facial muscles screamed tension. Even Gem sensed it, because the horse quivered and cocked his ears every time Kip touched him.

Had Kip talked to Janine again? Or was it some problem with Grace? The girl sat watching from the bleachers, her chin on her fist. She seemed oblivious to Tom Jacobs sitting beside her in rapt fascination.

Of course, it was plenty obvious whom Tom was watching. Sheridan doubted the man had taken his eyes off her mother since they were first introduced.

At the end of class, after the volunteers helped their clients walk the horses out to the pastures, Sheridan caught up with Kip and Ryan.

"So when are you gonna introduce me to your sister?" Ryan asked.

The edge behind Kip's grin might not have been obvious to Ryan, but Sheridan could read it a mile away.

"Before I'll let you date my sister, you better have a list of references as long as your arm."

"You're one of *those* big brothers, eh? No guy's ever gonna be good enough for Little Sis." Ryan punched Kip playfully in the shoulder.

Another forced smile. "Looks like the bus is loading. Best not keep Mr. Williams waiting."

"Next week, dude. See ya!" Ryan jogged toward the bus.

"Kip?" Sheridan caught his arm. "Want to tell me what's up?"

He dropped his chin to his chest. He started to say something and then seemed to think better of it. Taking her hand, he kissed it and said, "Nothin' for you to worry about, okay?"

Sheridan touched Kip's cheek. "Talk to me. Please."

Beneath her hand, his jaw muscles bunched with another unconvincing smile. A curtain fell across his eyes before he huffed and met her gaze full-on. "Let it go, okay? Everything's under control."

With a quick kiss on her cheek, he marched to the barn.

If that wasn't enough to make Sheridan believe Kip was avoiding her, the next few days convinced her. On class days he barely made eye contact. When she'd tried to talk to him at other times, he always seemed busy. Each evening Mom invited Kip and Tom to join them for dinner, and while Tom would accept, Kip made excuses. Either he wanted to spend more time training Jet, or he thought he should keep Ember in shape for when Nathan was ready to ride again. Or he had an errand in town, or . . .

When Sunday morning came, he declined a ride to church. Since Grace wasn't interested in "churchy stuff" either, Sheridan found herself driving Mom's Tahoe with

Nathan riding shotgun and Tom and her mother talking and laughing in the backseat.

Sheridan wondered all over again if she was wrong to entrust her heart to a man she'd met barely two months ago, a man with a past so troubled he might never overcome it.

At least she didn't worry about the new man in Mom's life. In many ways, Tom Jacobs reminded Sheridan of her dad—kind, tenderhearted, strong, wise. His Texas drawl was sweet to the ears, his easy-going nature like the calm in the eye of a storm.

Which, lately, was how Sheridan viewed her life—her emotions, anyway. She felt caught in a hurricane of anxiety, fearing that Kip would announce his departure any day. He had that look about him, like Jet pacing his stall just before a thunderstorm. Ready to jump. Ready to run.

Following worship, they enjoyed another Sunday lunch at Kingsley Station. Or rather, everyone else enjoyed lunch while Sheridan did little more than nudge her chicken teriyaki around the plate.

Mom laid her hand on Sheridan's arm. "Are you feeling okay? You haven't had much appetite all week."

Sheridan made herself take a bite of chicken. She chewed hard and forced it down with a gulp of water. "Maybe it's the heat. Can you believe it's nearly August?"

Nathan poured another dollop of ketchup across his home fries. "I'm thinkin' there's trouble in paradise. Does everyone notice who's *not* sitting in this booth with us?"

"Now, Nathan," Mom said. "I'm sure Kip only thought he should stay home with Grace."

If only that explained it. Sheridan choked down a forkful of rice pilaf. "Tom, are you still planning to head out this afternoon?"

"Much as I hate to, it's time to get back to the ranch."

Tom winked at Sheridan's mother. "But we have an agreement, right, Linda?"

Sheridan arched an eyebrow. "Agreement?"

Mom giggled. A rosy blush crept up her cheeks. "Tom's invited me to visit him in Nacogdoches during the break between summer and fall classes."

Nathan laughed in triumph. "Way to go, Mom!"

"Wow." Sheridan had no idea why tears suddenly sprang into her eyes. She was happy for her mother. Really, she was. "I, um—Nathan, could you let me out, please? I need to go powder my nose."

A perfect morning for a ride—if Kip had been in a better mood and it was Sheridan riding beside him and not his little sister. Nothing against Grace. In fact, he'd come to cherish every day he got to spend with her and the chance to know her better. But his heart ached for the woman he loved.

The woman whose heart he was destined to break.

"Good boy, Sundown." Grace reached forward to pat the gelding's neck. "I'm glad your hoof's all better."

The wooded trail narrowed between overhanging trees, and Kip reined Jet to the side to let Grace take the lead. When they entered a clearing, he trotted up even with Grace and then slowed to an easy walk. The horses seemed content to amble along, heads down, picking their way through the knee-high grass and stirring up grasshoppers and dragonflies. The trees hummed with the song of cicadas.

Grace glanced toward Kip. "You'd tell me if you heard from Mom again, wouldn't you?"

"Of course I would." Kip flicked the reins to chase off a horsefly. He probably checked his cell phone fifty times a day to make sure he hadn't missed a call. With every day that passed, he felt more certain Janine had abandoned Grace. It both worried and infuriated him. Surely the woman wasn't stupid or selfish enough to take off without making guardianship arrangements. How was Kip supposed to enroll Grace in school? What would he do if she needed medical care?

He halted Jet in the shade of a spreading oak and broached the subject he'd been avoiding for days now. "I was thinkin'. Until we get this sorted out, it might be a good idea if you and I went back to Texas—"

"I told you, I like it here just fine. Texas is nothin' but bad memories." Grace kicked out of her stirrups and slid to the ground. Letting Sundown graze, she stroked the horse's neck. "You're my new best friend, aren't you, fella?"

Probably a little late to tell her not to get too attached. If Janine didn't come back soon, Kip didn't see any way around returning to Texas. That was Janine's last known residence and where he'd most likely have to start if he wanted guardianship of Grace.

Why, Lord, why? He'd do anything to protect his sister, anything to make sure she had a good life. But leave Sheridan?

Anguish curdled Kip's stomach. His hands tightened into fists, the reins cutting into his flesh. Beneath him, Jet quivered and pranced.

Willing the tension from his limbs, he forced the hatred he felt for his mother deep down inside. Someday he'd have to deal with it once and for all, but more and more he had the sense that would be God's work, not his.

Because on his own, he didn't have the strength.

Chapter Twenty

"Linda, I've enjoyed my stay here more'n I ever expected." Tom Jacobs stood next to his pickup and rocked on his boot heels.

To Sheridan's eye, the big man looked like a nervous beau trying to decide whether it would be proper to give his date a goodbye kiss.

"My pleasure entirely." Mom's fingers fluttered at her nape. "I'll be looking forward to having you show me around Nacogdoches in a few weeks."

"And *that* will be *my* distinct pleasure." With a grin and a wink, Tom turned to Kip and pulled him into a fatherly hug. "You'll always have a friend in Texas, son, you hear?"

Kip lowered his eyes. "Thanks."

"Thanks again for bringing Ember," Nathan said. "I'm pretty sure I didn't pay you nearly what he's worth."

"Don't you worry about it." Tom gave Nathan's hand a firm shake before heaving a reluctant sigh. "Guess it's about time to hit the road."

"Drive safe," Kip said with a tip of his hat. One hand on Grace's shoulder, he stepped away from the pickup.

Sheridan signaled to Nathan with a sideways nod that they should give their mother some privacy. Taking her lead, he followed Sheridan to the porch. Sheridan turned in time to see Tom pull Mom close for a tender kiss on the cheek. Mom ducked her head with a happy smile that twisted Sheridan's heart.

Nathan nudged her. "Think we have a new stepdad in the picture?"

A shivery breath escaped Sheridan's lips. "Mom sure seems taken by him."

"Looks like the feeling's mutual."

They watched Tom steer his pickup and horse trailer through the gate and pretended not to notice when Mom brushed something wet from her cheek as she ambled toward the house.

Pausing on the steps, Mom called over her shoulder, "Grace, I'm of a mind to whip up a batch of brownies. You interested?"

Grace jogged over, leaving Kip standing in the empty lane.

Another elbow in the ribs from Nathan. "I think this is your cue to go see what's up with your gloomy cowboy." With a pointed glare, Nathan headed inside.

She supposed it wouldn't hurt to try—or maybe it would. Steeling herself for yet another rebuff, Sheridan caught up with Kip as he reached the cottage door. "Got a minute?"

He halted, one hand on the screen door handle. "Sure."

An ache formed at the base of her throat. She locked her arms across her ribcage. "Did I do something? Say something?"

He pulled off his Stetson and held it in front of his chest. "It isn't you, Sher. It's—"

"Please." She clenched her jaw. "Don't give me the old 'It's not you; it's me' line. We've talked all this out before—your family history, my fears. I thought we—" The words jammed behind her heart, pressing upward until she thought her chest would explode. "I thought you loved me."

His eyes closed for the briefest moment before he fixed his gaze on something in the distance. Then with a stiff sigh he gave her his eyes, but the look deep within them spoke his answer before the words ever left his mouth. "Some things aren't meant to be, Sher. Some things just aren't meant to be."

Wednesday evening came and still no word from Janine. How he'd get through the last two weeks of classes, Kip wasn't sure. But he'd made a commitment, and he felt bound and determined to see it through.

Finishing up with barn chores, he felt his cell phone vibrate. His stomach catapulted. He checked the Caller ID —Tom Jacobs—and tried to settle his breathing. "Hey, Tom. You make it home okay?"

"Nary a problem. Just called to see how you're doin'."

Kip tipped back his Stetson. "Any chance you know a good lawyer?"

"*That* came out of left field! This have somethin' to do with your little sister?"

"I think Janine's long gone. Grace and I may be heading back your way soon."

"Nothin' I'd like better, son. But your life there—you seemed so happy."

"Can't be helped. I owe it to my sister to look after her."

And he owed it to Sheridan and the Crosses to make sure his family problems didn't mess up their lives any more than they already had.

"I understand. I'll text you my attorney's name and number." Tom chuckled. "And listen, son, nothin' says you can't head on back to your sweetheart soon as you take care of business here."

"Yeah, I know." But he'd already made such a mess of things. Did he dare ask her to wait?

He'd barely stuffed the phone back into his pocket when it buzzed again. This time the caller registered anonymous. Warily he answered.

"Hi, son," Janine began. "I wanted to let you know I'll be back for Grace soon."

Kip tightened his grip on the phone. "Oh, yeah? Well, I'm not so sure I want you taking her. She's happy with me. And a lot better off than she was with you."

A pause. "Please don't do this, Kip. I'm her mother."

"Just now rememberin' that, are you?"

"I *never* forgot." Her voice shook. "Please, give me a chance to prove—"

"Daddy gave you all kinds of chances. Look where your empty promises got him—crushed beneath his own pickup when one of your stoned roadie friends ran him off the highway."

A muffled sob. "I'll regret your daddy's death till the day I die. I can't fix the past, but I'm tryin' to change the future." Her voice hardened. "Believe me or don't believe me. Just tell Grace I'll be there soon."

Panic clawed the back of Kip's neck. "*How* soon? Where exactly are you? What are you—"

A shuffling sound made him glance over his shoulder. The barn door bounced twice on its hinges. Just the wind, probably. Thunder rumbled in the distance. When he spoke into the phone again, he realized he was talking to dead air. Thumbing the disconnect button, he ground his teeth. He'd started out dreading he'd have to take over Grace's care. Now he was determined to do just that.

Nathan peered out the living room window as a lightning bolt zigzagged across the ink-black sky. "Looks like Kip's in for another rough night with Jet."

Sheridan bit her tongue. She'd gone from confused to hurt to downright angry that Kip could shut her out so easily. She flipped to the next page of her lesson plan notebook. School started in three weeks. About time she psyched herself up for another year.

At the next thunderbolt, Xena crept closer to Sheridan's chair. Beau already hid behind the sofa. "It's okay, girl. I'll protect you. Don't I always?"

"Biggest chihuahua I ever saw." Nathan plopped onto the sofa with a snicker. Out of the neck brace now, he moved much more freely.

Sheridan jotted some notes, then glanced at Nathan. "When do you head back to campus?"

"The fourteenth. My final semester! I am *so* ready to be done with school."

It eased Sheridan's mind knowing that after December Nathan would return home to stay, because her heart told her Kip would be long gone by then.

Another clap of thunder sent Xena bolting behind the sofa with Beau. The sound of doggy toenails gouging the polished wood floor quickly brought Mom from the kitchen.

"Beau. Xena. Out of there right this minute."

Sheridan rose. "Why don't I take the dogs up to my room? I was thinking about getting to bed early anyway."

"Works for me. I think Grace just went up to bed, and I'm headed that way myself."

With Mom grabbing Beau's collar and Sheridan clutching Xena's, they herded them upstairs. Sheridan changed into her sleep shirt, then switched off the light and drew back her curtain. Sheets of rain obscured the view, but she made out the dim glow of barn lights. She pictured Kip walking Jet up and down the aisle.

Lord, please, if there's any way You can change his heart . . .

She let the thought fade into the darkness and crawled into bed.

The storm faded at last, and Kip closed the door on Jet's stall. Dog tired, he trudged to the cottage, barely taking time to change into a dry T-shirt and boxers before sinking onto his pillow. The drip-drip-drip of rain from the eaves soon lulled him into a deep sleep.

Sometime in the early morning he stirred awake. Groggy, confused, he squinted at the digital clock—4:42. He lay there for a moment just listening. Long years of sleeping in barns and horse trailers had tuned his ears to any little sound that might indicate a horse in distress.

Nothing. Then . . .

Get up, Kip.

The words flashed through his brain like a neon sign. Something more than instinct, less than a spoken command.

He obeyed.

He shoved his legs into a fresh pair of jeans, stuffed his feet into socks and boots, and strode out to the barn. All quiet. He snapped the emergency flashlight off the wall charger and started down the left side, looking in on each sleepy horse. Coming up the other side, he stopped short at Sundown's stall.

Empty!

The stall gate was latched, which meant the horse didn't simply nudge it open and wander off. Kip immediately glanced where Sundown's halter should be hanging. Not there.

His stomach turned inside out. He raced outside, only then noticing the empty spot where his pickup should be. His rusty old horse trailer was missing as well.

Aw, Grace, what have you done?

The noise in the barn last night—Grace must have heard him on the phone with Janine. And how careless could a guy get? He'd grown so comfortable here that sometimes he didn't even take his keys out of the pickup—a habit which Grace had commented on more than once. Now, without a vehicle, he was stranded. Splashing through puddles, Kip scraped stiff fingers through his hair. Should he wake the Crosses? Call the sheriff's department?

Then he remembered the low water crossing. Grace knew only one way into town, and the crossing would be three feet underwater after last night's storm. If she were crazy enough to drive through it, the pickup would stall out halfway across, which meant Kip could still catch up with her and talk her out of this foolishness.

He darted into the tack room and grabbed Jet's saddle and bridle. Minutes later he climbed on the horse's back and galloped down the lane. Before Jet had a chance to balk at the cattle guard, Kip spurred him across in a smooth jump. The pavement clattered beneath Jet's metal shoes, and Kip strained to see the road ahead, hoping Jet's senses were sharper than his. Dawn was still an hour away, and with early morning fog swirling across the ground, it was hard to judge how far they'd traveled.

Red taillights broke through the mist. Kip pulled up on Jet's reins and leapt from the saddle. Water sloshed across his boots. The back of the horse trailer, stranded in the middle of the flooded crossing, loomed in front of him. Inside, Sundown whinnied. "Grace! You okay?"

"Kip?" She sounded scared, like she'd been crying.

He splashed through the water, fighting the weight against his legs. The pickup door stood open, but Grace wasn't inside. "Where are you, kiddo?"

"I'm sorry, Kip! I messed up so bad!"

He finally glimpsed her on the other side of the crossing. Fists at her temples, she paced at the edge of the lapping water.

Cursing the fog and darkness, he sloshed around the front of the pickup, only to be blinded by the sudden glare of headlights—a vehicle approaching from the other direction. The car skidded sideways and halted seconds before Kip recognized his mother's old green Dodge.

Janine climbed out the passenger door, shielding her eyes against the pickup's headlights. "Grace? Honey, what are you doin' middle of the road? I could've—"

"I'll never go back with you, Mom! Never!" Grace stumbled backward toward Kip, and he caught her by the waist. She spun around and clung to him, choking sobs tearing from her throat.

Janine edged forward, her face a mask of pain. "Please, let me explain—"

"What's to explain?" Keeping one eye on his mother, Kip gently untangled himself from Grace's arms. He positioned himself between her and Janine. "You thought you'd sneak in and take Grace before I could stop you."

"No! I just—" She shoved her hands into her tangled hair. "I know what it looks like, me showin' up like this. But after I talked to you last night, I couldn't sleep. I knew you'd be up early, and I thought if I told you face to face—"

"It's too late for your lame excuses. I'm taking Grace back to Texas, and I'm going to get you declared an unfit mother and get custody of her myself."

Quick, panicked breaths contorted Janine's mouth. She laced her fingers beneath her chin and muttered, "Please, Lord, give me strength."

The words stung Kip's ears. He inched closer to Grace. "Now you're *praying*? I never once heard you use the Lord's name in any way except as a curse."

Janine looked up, her voice as hard as the pavement beneath their feet. "You bet I'm praying. Praying like never before. Praying you'll finally forgive me. Praying you'll believe me when I say I'm gonna change. Because I am. I *will*."

"Don't listen to her, Kip." Grace seized his arm. "It's all talk. Like always. Promise you won't let her take me!"

Kip drew his sister to his side. "Don't worry, sis. She's not takin' you anywhere."

Yet even as he spoke, another Voice whispered through his mind: *Behold, I make all things new.*

Sheridan awoke to a wet nose against her cheek. Dark still shrouded the bedroom, but Xena's eyes shone with the reflected glow from the mercury light out back. Sheridan checked her clock—5:23. "Too early. Go back to sleep, girl."

Xena whined and dragged her warm tongue across Sheridan's ear. The dog bounded to the door and back to the bedside with an excited yip.

"Okay, okay." Sheridan threw aside the covers and pulled on her robe. When she opened the bedroom door, Xena barked and bolted for the stairs.

"Xena!"

Mom's door creaked open. "What's going on?"

Shuffling to the stairs, Sheridan waved a hand. "Xena wants out. Go back to sleep."

Xena was scratching and whining at the back door by the time Sheridan reached the kitchen. Then Beau joined her, apparently with the same urgency.

"Good grief, you two." Sheridan bullied her way between them to reach the knob. When she finally got the door open, both dogs tore across the yard, barking and running in circles, their noses in the air.

A chill raced up Sheridan's spine, her nerves instantly on alert. She scanned the grounds. It took her several seconds to notice, but then she saw it—the vacant space next to the cottage where Kip parked his pickup and horse trailer.

Gone?

Barefoot, she ran across the lane and pounded on Kip's door, already knowing he wouldn't answer. Maybe there'd been an emergency with one of the horses. She hurried to the barn and found the tack room door standing wide open, the fluorescent tubes overhead casting the room in a greenish glow. Immediately she noticed the empty racks. A couple of bridles and at least two saddles were missing, one of them Jet's Passier jumping saddle.

Dread seared Sheridan's throat. She tore through the barn, only to confirm what she already knew—both Jet's and Sundown's stalls stood empty.

"Oh, God, please, no!" Her mind screamed the one thing her heart didn't want to believe.

She hurried back to the house and sped to the foot of the stairs. "Mom! Mom!"

Mom appeared on the landing. "What is it, honey? Are the dogs okay?"

"Check Grace's room—*now!*"

Mom frowned in puzzlement but did as she was asked. In the meantime, Nathan roused and came into the hallway. "What's all the racket about?"

"She's not here," Mom called from the landing. "Her suitcase is gone, too."

Sheridan spun in a small circle, trying to make sense of it all. Her gaze landed on the hall storage bench, where she and Mom always dropped their purses. Both purses stood open, the wallet contents strewn across the bench. Sheridan rushed over. Driver's licenses, credit cards—all those items remained untouched. The only thing missing was the money.

An icy calmness crackled in Sheridan's veins. A little voice inside her head sang a mocking refrain: *Only a fool would trust a stranger.*

Kip—betray them? He wouldn't!

Unless that was the plan from the start—get established here, gain their sympathies—and Sheridan's love—with a sob story about a troubled past. Bring in the dysfunctional mother and poor, innocent sister, and when everyone least expected it, rob them blind.

A guttural sob choking her, Sheridan sank to her knees in front of the bench. "Nathan, call the sheriff."

Kip hauled in a breath and blew it out. "All right, you've got one chance to explain. And don't you even think of lying."

Janine's shoulders caved. She backed up until she leaned against the Dodge's right front fender. With a shuddering sigh, she mouthed a silent *Thank you, Jesus.* "Clyde kickin' me out was a wakeup call," she began. "I never felt so scared and alone in all my life. Once I got sober enough to notice how Grace had started acting out, I knew I had to pull myself together before I ruined her life, too."

Grace harrumphed. "Too late for that."

"Let her have her say." One hand lifted, Kip stepped toward his mother. "That's when you decided to look for me?"

Janine nodded. "No way I could get straight without help. But I needed to know Grace was with someone I could trust."

"So . . . all this time . . . you've been drying out?"

"That, and a whole lot more. I got me an AA sponsor. I been going to church. I been leanin' on the Lord like you wouldn't believe—prayin' my heart out, beggin' Him to heal the hurt I've caused my daughter . . . and my son."

Kip palmed his forehead. His heart cried for God's help, because he really wanted to believe her. "If I'd known—if you'd have told me from the start—"

"You'd have listened?" Janine sent him a sad, knowing smile. "No, son, I'd already burned too many bridges with you. I knew I'd have to prove myself before you'd ever trust me again."

Eyes squeezed shut, Kip let the past play out across the stage of his mind—the nights when Daddy tucked him into bed because "Mommy's got the flu," the times he'd waited outside the school building till nearly dark because his mother "got stuck in traffic." Only years later did he figure out "the flu" was a euphemism for being staggering drunk, and "getting stuck in traffic" meant Mom had spent the afternoon nursing tequila sunrises while watching her favorite honky-tonk band rehearse.

His fingers curled into his palms until his knuckles ached. Warring emotions battered his heart. Condemn her? Forgive her? *Trust her?*

God, help!

"Kip." Sheridan's voice. She was here?

And then another sound—sirens.

"Please, please forgive me, Kip!"

Sheridan was asking forgiveness? His brain struggled to keep up as he turned toward her. She stood at the water's edge, the first fingers of dawn lighting her pale hair with a soft glow. Desperation etched her face.

She stretched a hand toward him. "When I found you and Grace gone, I— Oh, Kip, I should never have doubted you."

The sirens grew to an ear-splitting scream. Blue and red strobes pulsed through the fog. The sirens stopped suddenly. Doors slammed, and four uniformed deputies approached, right hands resting on their holstered weapons.

All at once, Kip understood.

Could this day get any worse?

Chapter Twenty-One

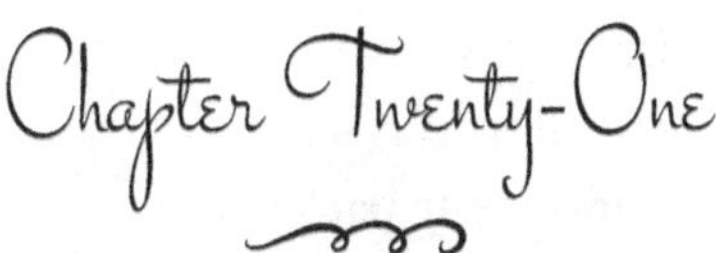

Sheridan leaned in the kitchen doorway as one of the deputies questioned Grace. Two others had taken Kip and his mother aside to interview them privately. Precautionary, the lead deputy had explained. With a minor involved, they couldn't take any chances.

"I'm so sorry, Mrs. Cross." Grace scraped a fresh tissue across her wet face. "I didn't mean to steal from you. I'm sorry for taking Sundown, too, but I couldn't stand the thought of leaving him." She hiccuped. "I just wanted to get away before my mom came for me."

"I understand, sweetie." Sheridan's mother patted Grace's arm. Only as Sheridan was putting her purse in order after they returned had she found Grace's hastily scribbled note. In it she'd thanked them for all they'd done and promised to repay the money as soon as she possibly could.

The deputy closed his notebook and rose. "I think I've got all the facts straight now. Far as I'm concerned, this was all a big misunderstanding."

"I want to go check on Sundown." Grace pushed away

from the table. "And then . . . I guess I'd better talk to my mom."

Sheridan's mother offered a sympathetic smile. "Try to remember, she did what she did because she loves you."

"I know. I just wish she would have trusted me enough to explain before she left." Grace heaved a tired sigh, and the deputy escorted her out the back door.

When it closed behind them, Sheridan sank into the chair next to her mother. "Trust. That's what this is all about, isn't it?" She let her head fall onto her folded arms. "How could I have been so stupid? How could I ever distrust Kip?"

"It was an honest reaction, honey. Kip doesn't blame you."

"Then why won't he talk to me?" She'd never forget the look in his eyes when the deputies arrived. Weary, confused, forsaken.

Mom draped an arm across Sheridan's shoulders. "Remember what I said once, about how there's a hurting little boy inside Kip? Whether he knows it or not, he needs you now more than ever."

Sheridan lifted her head. She sat up and brushed away her tears. "I won't lose him, Mom. I'm going to fight for him with everything I've got."

With her mother's smile to strengthen her, she marched outside and across the yard. As she neared the cottage, the deputies were just sliding into their cars to leave. She hesitated only a moment before rapping once on the cottage door and then striding into Kip's small sitting room. With only a quick glance at Mrs. Lawton, sitting on the sofa, Sheridan stood before Kip in the easy chair. "We have to talk."

"Yeah, guess we do." He sat forward.

Clearing her throat, his mother rose. "I got some talkin' to do, too—if Grace will listen now."

Sheridan shook off her own burdens long enough to cast Mrs. Lawton a concerned smile. "I think she will. You'll probably find her in the barn with Sundown."

When the door closed behind the woman, Sheridan knelt beside Kip's chair. She longed to hold him in her arms, but he looked so beaten down that she feared the slightest touch would cause him to draw back. "Look at me, Kip. Please."

Slowly, slowly, he swiveled his head toward her, but he kept his eyes lowered. "I never meant for my troubles to bleed over onto you and your family. I'll be packed up and out of here before—"

"You will do no such thing." The force behind her words made her voice shake. "I love you, Kip, and I won't let you go."

He glanced up at her with disbelieving eyes. "You still love me? After what I just put you through?"

"It wasn't your fault. You were only trying to protect Grace. I'll never be able to forgive myself for not trusting you."

"Don't, Sher." Pain etched his face. "It's okay. I understand."

She sank back on her heels, a tear sliding down her cheek. "See, that's the thing. You understand my lack of trust. I understand yours. And yet here we are, two messed-up people in love. What are we going to do about that?"

Kip drew in a long breath that seemed to go all the way to his boot soles. "For a while now I've had this voice runnin' through my head. It keeps saying the same thing: *The past doesn't have to repeat itself.* Guess that means we both need to get better about trusting."

Sheridan reached for his hand. "Guess it does."

Something like laughter, something like tears, bubbled up from Kip's throat. He captured Sheridan's hands, pulling them into his chest. She nestled into his embrace, chills rushing up her spine has he brushed the curl behind her ear with a gentle kiss. "Forgive me," he murmured, "for ever thinking I could leave you."

"You wouldn't have gotten very far." Sheridan pressed her cheek into the warmth at his neck. "Maybe you haven't noticed, but once I set my mind to something, I can be pretty tenacious."

Easing her to one side, he slid off the chair and onto his knees until they were eye to eye. He clutched both her hands in his. "I don't think I can live without you, Sher, and I never want to find out. I've got some things to work out with Grace and my mother, but . . . will you wait for me?"

She cocked an eyebrow. "Is that a proposal?"

Kip stroked Sheridan's left hand. "I wish I had a ring to give you to seal the deal."

Her gaze mellowed. "I don't need a ring. All I need is right here in front of me."

Pausing next to her car door, Janine brushed wetness from her face. "You take good care of my girl, all right?"

"You know I will, Jan—Mom." Forgiveness, Kip was learning, could be a two-steps-forward-one-step-back kind of thing, not unlike what his mother faced now that she'd committed herself to a rehab program.

They'd spent the last several days working with an attorney in Charlotte who'd arranged for Kip to take temporary guardianship of Grace. She'd be living at the farm now and starting high school in Kingsley in a couple of weeks.

Shyly, awkwardly, Janine held out her arms to Kip for a goodbye hug, which he couldn't refuse. She still smelled of tobacco, but she promised she was cutting back. After a tearful embrace with Grace, Janine climbed into her old green sedan and drove away.

Kip tucked Grace under his arm. "Just so you know, I intend to be highly overprotective. No drinking, no smoking, no fast cars. And no dating till you're thirty-five."

Grace giggled and twirled out of his reach. "If you ask me, *you're* the one who needs a chaperone."

Kip glanced toward the Crosses' back porch, where Sheridan smiled and waved. "You might be right about that."

He jogged across the lane and met Sheridan on the lawn.

"You okay?" she asked softly.

"Better'n okay." He grinned and drew her close for a kiss. "Come out to the barn with me. I got a surprise for you."

She shot him a skeptical frown. "You know how I feel about surprises."

"Trust me. You'll like this one." He took her hand and together they started across the yard.

Halfway to the barn she glanced at him sideways. "Kip, you're limping."

"It's nothing." He took a few more steps and sucked air between his teeth.

"Nothing! You're obviously in pain." Inside the barn, she made him sit down on a hay bale. "Get your boot off and let me take a look."

"Ow. Yeah, maybe you should." He pried his foot out of his left boot and wiggled his toes.

Kneeling, Sheridan peeled off his sock. Her warm hands against his skin sent ripples up his spine. "I don't see anything. Where does it hurt?"

"Hard to tell. Maybe there was a pebble in my boot. Shake it out, why don't you?"

Sheridan gave the boot a firm shake, and a tiny velvet pouch spilled out. "What in the world—"

Kip bit down on the inside of his cheek. "Well, glory be. How'd that get in there?"

"Kip Lorimer—" Sheridan loosened the drawstrings and emptied the pouch into her palm. A shimmering diamond ring slid out. "Oh, Kip!"

"I figure I'll have to work for your mother at least another six months to pay for it. And then I'm plannin' to slip a little gold band on your finger right next to it. Does that sound okay with you?"

Sheridan sank onto her haunches and narrowed one eye. "Hmmm. What's your job experience? Do you have any references?"

"Just this." Kip drew her into his arms and pressed one hand against the small of her back. With the other, he cradled her head as he moved in for a long, slow kiss.

Breathless, Sheridan smiled up at him with a look of love that seared his heart. "That settles it, cowboy. You're hired!"

Are you ready for the next book in the series?
Look for Nathan and Filipa's love story in book 2,
A Horseman's Gift

If you enjoyed *A Horseman's Heart*, please spread the word among your reader friends and wherever you share about books on Facebook, Goodreads, Instagram, or other social media.

Reviews are always deeply appreciated. A review doesn't have to be lengthy or eloquent, just a few brief words sharing your honest impressions. Reviews and personal recommendations are the best ways to help authors get discovered by new readers.

To receive regular updates about Myra Johnson's books and special events, subscribe to her newsletter (signup form on website, http://myrajohnson.com/newsletter-signup/).

Visit Myra online:
www.myrajohnson.com

Myra Johnson writes emotionally layered Christian romance that explores love, loss, and the healing power of faith. Whether set in contemporary small towns, ranch country, or the struggles of the past, her stories reflect a deep compassion for the wounded heart and a reverence for family and faith. Readers can also expect to find dogs, cats, and horses regularly wandering through the pages of her stories.

Myra's novels have received numerous honors, including Christian Retailing's Best for historical fiction, the National Excellence in Romance Fiction Awards, and recognition from ACFW, the Selah Awards, the HOLT Medallion, and others. Her goal is to bring readers along on her characters' hope-filled journeys toward redemption and lasting love.

A native Texan, Myra has also called Oklahoma and the Carolinas home, but she and her husband of over 50 years are happily settled back in the Lone Star State enjoying wildflowers, Tex-Mex, and real Texas barbecue. The Johnsons have two beautiful daughters married to faithful Christian men, plus seven grandchildren and an adorable great-granddaughter. They share their home on the edge of the Texas Hill Country with a couple of pampered rescue dogs and one sassy cat who thinks he's the boss of everyone.

To receive regular updates about Myra's books and other news, be sure to subscribe to her newsletter (signup form on website).

Find Myra online:
www.myrajohnson.com

facebook.com/MyraJohnsonAuthor

instagram.com/mjwrites

threads.net/@mjwrites

bookbub.com/authors/myra-johnson

goodreads.com/MyraJohnsonAuthor

pinterest.com/mjwrites

x.com/MyraJohnson

Novels by Myra Johnson

Find the complete list at Myra's website,
www.MyraJohnson.com

MISSOURI LOVE STORIES
Autumn Rains
Romance by the Book
Where the Dogwoods Bloom

HORSEMEN OF CROSS ROADS FARM
A Horseman's Heart
A Horseman's Gift
A Horseman's Hope

WEST TEXAS SWEETHEARTS
Rancher for the Holidays
Worth the Risk

HILL COUNTRY HAVEN
Her Hill Country Cowboy
Hill Country Reunion
The Rancher's Redemption
Their Christmas Prayer

THE RANCHERS OF GABRIEL BEND

The Rancher's Family Secret

The Rebel's Return

The Rancher's Family Legacy

MONTANA MERCIES

A Steadfast Companion

His Unexpected Grandchild

One Glance of Your Eyes

FLOWERS OF EDEN HISTORICAL SERIES

The Sweetest Rain

Castles in the Clouds

A Rose So Fair

TILL WE MEET AGAIN HISTORICAL SERIES

When the Clouds Roll By

Whisper Goodbye

Every Tear a Memory

CONTEMPORARY WOMEN'S FICTION

All She Sought

One Imperfect Christmas

The Soft Whisper of Roses

NOVELLAS

The Oregon Trail Romance Collection: Settled Hearts

Designs on Love

Lifetime Investment

www.ingramcontent.com/pod-product-compliance
Lightning Source LLC
Chambersburg PA
CBHW032000180726
48283CB00008B/2504